"This is an inspiring and interesting book. As a Christian, the story touched me. As a Christian businessperson, it challenged me and made me want to better use the platform that God has given me."
Mr. W. T. (Tobin) Cassels, III
President, Southeastern Freight Lines, Inc.

"I heartily recommend this book to help people effectively share the Gospel with their coworkers. The fact that it is in a novel format makes the reading easier and takes the theology and vision quickly to the heart of the reader. This book could impact and expand Marketplace Ministry the way the *Left Behind* series brought the return of our Lord back into the focus of believers and seekers alike."
Chuck Milian, Senior Pastor
Crossroads Fellowship

"A mind-tingling, quick-reading, spiritual novel. The author has an idea...planted by God, I think...of how the most spectacular revival in history may occur. And it might not be too far away. Read this fictional novel now...it may not be fiction for long."
Mr. Jess Duboy, President
Duboy Automotive Advertising Group

"This book encourages me to live a powerful, fruitful Christian life in today's business world. It reminds me that Jesus' eternal measure of success satisfies the soul dramatically more than worldly success."
Mr. Frank Holding, President
First Citizens Bank

"Mark Cress is a shining example of what I like to call 'evangelism entrepreneurs'—folks who understand the Gospel is unchanging, but the way we go about penetrating the culture with the Gospel must adjust to given cultures. His passion for awakening and evangelism are evident in this work. May God begin a mighty revival in our lifetime!"

Dr. Alvin L. Reid, Associate Dean for Proclamation,
Bailey Smith Chair of Evangelism,
Southeastern Baptist Theological Seminary

"Mark Cress has captured the essence of God's present movement in and through Christian business owners and leaders in the marketplace. We are seeing microcosmic examples of this huge story every day across the world.

"Tears filled my eyes several times as I read the story of William J. Brantley, a man much like many others that I have come to know and revere as they carry the Cross with them to work each day. Can revival come on this scale? How big is your God?"

Mr. Buck Jacobs, Founder & Chairman
The C-12 Group, LLC

the third
Awakening

A NOVEL

MARK CRESS

LANPHIER
PRESS

The Third Awakening
by Mark Cress
Copyright ©2004 Mark Cress

ISBN 0-9762151-0-1
For Worldwide Distribution
Printed in the U.S.A.

Second Printing

Lanphier Press
U.S.A.
www.LanphierPress.org

Table of Contents

Acknowledgments

It is wonderful to be able to confess that this book represents a collaborative effort of many. For as far back as I can remember, I have always been an entrepreneur. It is the way God created me and thankfully the way my precious Mom & Dad, Ann & John Cress, nurtured me. Further, God gave me Linda, the perfect entrepreneur's wife, who is a tremendous encourager, and then he gave us two wonderful daughters, Ashley & Avery, to add another layer of love and encouragement.

As a general rule, it usually takes a group of able and talented people to help a real entrepreneur get anything done. Therefore, it would be totally dishonest for me to say that I wrote every word of this book or even a minority of the words. In this project, I would be best seen as the conductor of a great orchestra who happened to write a piece of music and then had the privilege of directing a group of very talented musicians as they brought the notes on the page to life. God simply gave me the idea for this book, the joy of overseeing the process, and the resources to bring it to press, which ultimately allowed it to make its way into your hands.

Our staff at Corporate Chaplains of America put in many long hours on this project, especially Jeff Hilles, Dwayne Reece, Cindy Rice, and José Rondón. Technical knowledge of engineering processes was provided by Josh Duke. Dr. Alvin Reid advised me on the history of worldwide spiritual awakenings. My friend and theology professor from my seminary days, Dr. Danny Akin, offered encouragement and theological advice. Also, thanks go out to Jess Duboy, Ron Duke, Rick Butler, George King, Buck Jacobs, Paul Carlisle, Jim and Agnes Goldston, Kent Humphreys, Dr. David Jeremiah, Bob Pettus, Tobin Cassels, Pat Flood, Chuck Milian, Frank Holding, Rob Estes, and Zig Ziglar for special assistance and encouragement. I would also be totally remiss to leave out a special thanks to our field chaplain team. Without their contribution in the field, none of this would be possible. Like I said, it takes many talented musicians to pull off a great symphony.

As we prayed about someone to assist us with fictional writing, we contacted publishers for leads of great technical writers to aid in developing the fictional story from our outline. Without hesitation, Brian Banashak of Evergreen Press recommended Paul Murphy for the project. He had recently published Paul's book, *The 13th Apostle*. After reviewing the book I flew to Detroit to meet with Paul and knew immediately that God had brought us together for this project. Kathy Banashak served as our general editor.

The pure motivation for this work is that you might see Jesus, the hope of glory, as the only One who can bring spiritual awakening to millions around the planet and that you might claim Him as your personal Lord and friend. He is our hope for life here on earth and later for all of eternity. So thanks most of all to You, Jesus, my God, my strength, my sustainer, my Redeemer, my friend. I place this in your hands, use it as you see fit.

Mark Cress
November 18, 2004

Introduction

For years I have wondered why God has waited so long to usher in a Third Great Awakening. One of my heroes of the mid-1800s was a business guy in New York City named Jeremiah Lanphier. Like many of my Christian business friends today, he longed to see a great movement of God in the business community. Little did he know that the simple prayer meetings he started alone during his workplace lunch hour would ultimately result in more than 50,000 people a day praying for revival. Further, I doubt he ever thought these prayers would usher in what Perry Miller of Harvard would later refer to as "The Event of the Century"—an awakening formally referred to as "The Layman's Prayer Revival." Scholars estimate that possibly a million people came to Christ as a result.

One day I was having a telephone conversation with my dear friend Dr. Paul Carlisle about the idea for this book. We talked about some of the facts that I had received from our mutual friend, Professor of Evangelism Dr. Alvin Reid. Big Al, as I like to refer to him, basically confirmed my frustration that in spite of the fact that there had been some mighty movements of God since the late 1800s, there had certainly not been a third great awakening. Like me, however, he felt certain that there would be one in our lifetime. As Paul and I talked, I became firm in my opinion that as Christians, myself included, we often place God in a box, and thus put limits or parameters on our expectations of what He might accomplish through us as believers. Paul immediately, though kindly and gently, rebuked my thoughts on the subject as only a true friend can. He spoke the truth to me that man cannot put God in a box at all, that the box is in our heads and that God is truly only limited by the imagination and ability of our prayer lives.

This sent my thoughts to a statement I had recently heard, that each week over 10,000 people in China are coming to Christ. That means there are over a half million new converts coming to Jesus every year from this continent alone. This caused me to think about what they may be praying for, as new converts. Without question they must be asking God for revival. I doubt that there are that many people in the U.S. praying for revival at any given time, but I have become convinced that these new Chinese converts are doing so fervently. Then the thought hit me, if a revival were to break out in China and only ten percent of the population were to come to Christ in a relatively short period of time, the number of new converts, totaling more than 150 million, would constitute a great awakening in and of itself. This groundswell of new believers could light the torch of a worldwide event unparalleled in the history of the Church.

I sensed God wanted me to write about this concept, but I did not know where to start. I wrote the draft of an initial chapter, but it was so awful that I told our staff unless God were to give me a better way to tell this story, the idea could not possibly be from Him, and that we would abandon the book completely. I prayed about the whole matter one last time and left it in God's hands.

Within 48 hours, a complete paradigm shift occurred in my thinking about the book. I saw that it was not to be an academic work of convincing facts at all. It was to be a fast and fun fictional read that would spark imagination.

From that point forward, the book became a collaboration that came together much faster and more smoothly than anyone on our team could have ever imagined. Over and over we hear economic news reports about the Chinese people's fascination with our free enterprise system and business models. It is through the workplace that I am convinced we will see this next great revival sweep the world. We trust you will enjoy this book and join us in our prayer for and belief that God will bring about, in whatever manner He sees fit, a true *Third Awakening*.

Chapter 1

The Day That Changed Everything

The well-intended, but certainly unmelodic refrains of assembled friends and caring staff of Sunnyside Assisted Living Community floated through the air in the common dining room, "Happy birthday, dear Idella, happy birthday to you."

Idella Brantley stared at the white frosted cake with the number 91 shaped by the lit candles as she thought, *I know they mean well, but reaching 91 is nothing to brag about. It is really much ado about nothing, but of course I don't want to hurt their feelings.*

She smiled and looked at those gathered around her as they encouraged her to blow out the candles. They laughed when she asked if anyone had a hair dryer before she heartily blew them all out with several quick puffs to the applause of everyone.

"Speech!" someone called out. Others joined in and encouraged her to say something.

"Well, somebody had better cut the cake so you all can get back to what you were doing," she jokingly replied. "However, I can't thank each of you enough for your kindness since I came to Sunnyside. I'm sure many of you remember my first days here two years ago. I guess you would say that I came kicking and screaming, but each of you have helped me to understand this was the best move for me. No one hovers over me like I was afraid they would," she sighed. "You all have helped me realize that change can be good. Thank you for putting up with me. I must say that God was smiling when He led me here. Now let's eat."

Just then a local florist walked into the room holding a huge floral arrangement containing just about every flower Idella could imagine. After the cook removed the cake, he carefully placed the large vase on the table in front of her.

Idella reached out with her bony right hand and carefully opened the envelope. Someone offered, "I'll bet I can guess who those are from."

"And you would be right," she replied as she read the card. "Wish I could be there. I know you under-stand. All my love. BB." She rolled her eyes when she reached the signature.

"That little stinker," she said. She looked up at all those gathered around her. "He knows how much I despise nicknames, and he goes ahead and signs it with his initials."

"Oh, you know how much he loves you, Idella," Clair Chapman, her closet friend at Sunnyside, reassured her.

"I know, Clair, but I guess he's always been a little

stubborn. William is the brightest star in my life. I've always known that he was special. Although the day he became a major part of my life was the worst day anyone could imagine, it turned out to be the best thing that ever happened to me.

"I know, I know." She raised her hands to acknowledge all those in front of her. "you've all heard the story far too many times, and when I reminisce you are so kind as to permit me to tell the story again and again. But not today. I just want a piece of that cake so that we can all enjoy the moment together. And I'll have a glass of that sparkling grape juice just to live on the edge a little for one day. Thanks to all of you for a nice party."

Several hours later, Idella sat alone in her two-bedroom apartment in her favorite chair, admiring the floral arrangement her precious William had wired her. Idella fingered the card she had received earlier that afternoon and leaned back with a satisfied smile on her face.

She thought back on that horrid day almost 40 years earlier when William became a permanent part of her household. She had been widowed for almost five years at the time. Clinton, her husband, had been the town drunk. Richfield was located in the most southwestern corner of Virginia, a quaint little village where everyone knew everyone else's business—and they definitely knew Clinton's. He had not been a mean drunk; in fact those that knew him well called him a loveable drunk. He did not have a mean bone in his body, but he could

3

not control his consumption of alcohol, which eventually destroyed his liver. He died at the age of 48, leaving Idella with nothing but the house and a small Social Security pension.

They had one child, Roger, who left home as soon as he could, not only because he was embarrassed by his father's reputation, but also because he wanted to see the world. While Roger was in the Navy, he married Danielle Waverly, a Hospitalman One 1st Class Petty Officer, a position she was proud to hold. Two years later, they had their only child, William, whom they loved and cherished.

Both were hard workers, and so it was only on rare occasions that Idella got to see her grandchild. Usually at Thanksgiving or Christmas, as well as once during the summer, they would make the drive to her house from wherever they were stationed, each time forcing Idella and the boy to renew their relationship. It was difficult for all of them, but that was how it had to be.

It was after one such visit over the Christmas holidays that these family get-togethers were brought to an abrupt halt. Idella, Roger, and Danielle had said their good-byes, but for the first time, William, who was almost five, did not want to go. He had decided that he wanted to stay with Grammy, not so much for her sake as it was he did not like the long drive and always grew restless in the car. She smiled as she recalled him saying, "I don't like riding in the car. Can't I just stay here?"

Out of the mouths of babes they say—and his request was just an inkling of things to come, Idella

4

thought as she leaned back in her chair and rested her eyes.

———

She would never forget hearing the emergency vehicle sirens the night William had fruitlessly pleaded to remain at her house. A half hour later, she heard a knock at her front door. It was the local Chief of Police, Tom Logan, a man she had gotten to know quite well due to the many times she had to retrieve Clinton from the police station. For some reason, the police never filed any drunk and disorderly charges against her husband; they just called Idella. Embarrassed, she would go pick him up, bring him home, and put him to bed. The year before he died, her excursions to the jail had become almost a routine.

"Is there a problem, Thomas?" she asked as she opened the screen door to let the policeman in.

Chief Logan pursed his lips as he said, "Idella, there's been an accident, and you'll need to come with me."

Idella's knees buckled as Logan reached out to steady her.

She blurted out, "Roger! Danielle! William! No! It can't be! Not my children!" She sucked in a deep breath and grabbed the door frame to steady herself. Through clenched teeth she asked, "How bad is it, Thomas? Are they..." she stopped, unable to inquire further. She looked pleadingly into his eyes.

The tears forming in his eyes told her it was worse than she had even anticipated.

"Roger, is he..."

The chief placed his hand on her shoulder, "I'm afraid Roger didn't make it, and they've taken Danielle and the boy to the hospital."

"William?"

"Not a scratch," he shook his head in disbelief, "not a scratch. His seatbelt saved him. Come with me, and I'll take you to the hospital."

As they sped through the night, the chief explained that Roger had hit an oil slick on Weaver Road, causing the car to skid and roll over an embankment.

"An elderly couple passing by called 911," the chief continued. "Those poor people felt so helpless because they couldn't get down the steep slope to help. When the rescue squad finally got to the car, Roger had already passed on, but Danielle was barely alive. And there was little William—he was still hanging by his seatbelt, a little dazed, but not a mark on him. When they pulled him out of the car, he told the EMT, Susan Holtz, that she needn't worry about his Mommy and Daddy because they were going to meet God and to see Jesus." The chief's voice broke as he finished his story.

When they pulled in front of the emergency room doors, he took hold of Idella's hand. "Idella, I know how faithful you are to God and only He knows how much you've already been through with Clint. I know that losing Roger and possibly Danielle will be hard for you to bear. You know you can count on me and my guys and especially the church. I pray that we can all be a comfort to you."

Idella patted his hand and forced a smile. "The Lord will help me through this. Roger is with Him now and may be speaking to Clinton for the first time in years. My son fulfilled God's purpose here; I just don't know what it was. My only prayer is that Roger didn't suffer and that Danielle is in no pain."

"Danielle's out cold. If it's any comfort, Susan said that Roger was killed instantly. William's going to need you more than ever. Does he have any other kin?"

"I don't think so," she replied. "Danielle was an only child and her parents were killed in an airplane crash on their way to see her when she graduated from Great Lakes. So I guess it just leaves the three of us right now."

Five minutes later, inside the bustling emergency room, they learned that the doctors were working feverishly to keep Danielle alive. They wanted William to remain overnight for observation.

"When can I see William?" Idella asked.

Wilma Thurmond, the head nurse, walked Idella toward her grandson's room. "Idella, I took the liberty to call Pastor Harrelson. I apologize if I overstepped my bounds."

"Not at all, Wilma. You and I have been going to the same church for I don't know how long. I would have done the same for you. Thanks. Now to William. Is there anything else that I should know? Has he been told about Roger?"

"Susan seems to think he knows, but I'm not so sure," Nurse Thurmond told her. "I wish I knew what to say to you—but when it comes to my close friends— well, I'm just not very good at figuring out what to say, not very good at all."

When they arrived at William's room, Idella turned to her friend and gave her a warm hug. "You've done enough already, Wilma. Just pray for Danielle and William, and we'll make it through this."

Idella was surprised to see William sitting up in bed with his red hair matted against his skin, the usual wisp dangling across his forehead. His expressionless stare gave no indication that he even knew that she was there.

Idella reached out and brushed the unruly lock of hair back into place. After putting her arms around him, she caressed his left hand. Since William was born, she found that rubbing his hands in this manner calmed him, though tonight she wanted it to only show him that she was there no matter where he was at the moment.

At midnight, Pastor Harrelson arrived with Nurse Thurmond and called Idella outside William's room to tell her that Danielle had died on the operating table. Idella nodded, acknowledging their presence and the horrid news, and went right back to William's side. The good pastor stayed with her most of the night as she rocked the newly orphaned boy, all the while trying to envision their future.

Pastor Harrelson finally broke the silence. "I know this may be too soon, Idella, but you are going to take the boy into your home, are you not?"

Without hesitation, Idella replied, "Of course. Whatever would give you the impression I wouldn't?"

"I just wanted to make sure we were on the same page, that's all. He needs you as much as you need God right now. The church has already started a prayer chain for the two of you. As for me, I'll stay as long as you need me."

"Thank you," she mouthed as she continued to rock William while she hummed a song she used to sing to his father.

———•◦•◦•———

Three months later, Idella sat in William's bedroom by his bed while he went to sleep as she had done every night since he had come to live with her. It was a little before 9 p.m., and she was ready for bed, dressed in a blue-ribbed bathrobe and slippers, which had both seen better days. She rocked in the chair Clinton had given her when Roger was born. William was resting well, as he had since the accident, and seemed to be at peace here. She reached out and gently repositioned that unruly lock of red hair. He stirred at her tender touch and then settled back into a sound sleep. She took his small hand and placed it between hers and gently caressed the back of it.

He's going to be quite the handsome young man his father was, she thought as she leaned back in her chair. *That red hair and cherubic freckled face will drive the girls wild.* She quietly chuckled.

The last few months had been a blur to Idella. Without Pastor Harrelson and his flock, it would have been an even more difficult transition. He arranged for Idella and William to be picked up every Sunday for services, as well as any other function the church had.

Remembering back over this time, she thought, *The*

church has helped William considerably in making the adjustment. Losing one's mother and father has to be the worst event in anyone's life, especially at this age, but he seems to be reconciled that they are in heaven. She sighed as she reflected on her one concern—William's invisible friend.

The night of the wreck, Chief Logan had told her that William's first words to the paramedics were that Mommy and Daddy were in heaven with God. More puzzling was that Danielle was not yet dead. William's only explanation was that while he was hanging by his seatbelt, Big Mike had told him not to worry because God would be taking them to heaven with Him. The doctors thought that the appearance of Big Mike was the result of a slight concussion and that William had imagined the whole episode. At least that was the reason they gave for keeping him in the hospital overnight.

But Big Mike had not gone away; he continued to be William's friend. According to William, Big Mike was in his room every night, not saying anything, just smiling. Big Mike rarely said anything. Idella checked with a psychologist at church to see if having an invisible friend was a sign that there was something seriously wrong. He assured her that many children William's age had invisible friends and told her not to worry. "Let's see how long it lasts," he said. "Usually they grow out of this stage. It could be just months or maybe even a year, but there will come a point when you will ask where Big Mike is, and William will tell you that he was just an invisible friend. He might even say that he is too old to have a friend like that because he has new friends at school or church. Let's just wait and see, Idella. Let's not make something out of nothing."

Even with the doctor's reassurance, Idella could not help but worry. However, just before his sixth birthday, when she asked where Big Mike was, William responded, "He's gone back to heaven because I don't need him anymore." That was not quite the way the psychologist said it would happen, but what could one expect from a precocious child?

———————

Several years passed and William was turning into a principled young boy. Idella gave Pastor Harrelson and the church credit for that. They included him in every youth activity the church offered, and William absorbed what he learned at Hope Sanctuary like a sponge. *I wish he would act like that at school,* she caught herself thinking many times during his primary school years.

William did not seem interested in formal education and squeaked by doing as little as possible. No matter how strict Idella became, he showed little or no interest until fourth grade. That was when Miguel Estrada became his substitute teacher for a month at the end of the school year. For the entire month it was, "Mr. Estrada said this...Mr. Estrada did that...." There were times when Mr. Estrada seemed to have taken the place of Big Mike. But the upside was that William was finally turned on to school. His grades improved from a little less than average to the highest marks Mr. Estrada could give.

What a turn around it was, but Idella worried that

the next year's teacher would not be able to take the place of Mr. Estrada and then William would slip back into his old ways. Fortunately that did not happen. William became an exemplary student, eventually ending his senior year by earning valedictory honors at Richfield High School and being voted "Most Likely to Succeed" by his classmates. But Idella discovered from some of his friends that the honor was not because he had raised thousands of dollars to support Mr. Estrada's world mission work or that he worked various jobs to help support his grandmother. It seemed that his fellow students were most impressed by the fact that William, as Student Council president, had been able to convince the school administration to put soda vending machines in various places around the school building. *That sounds like William. He loves his Diet Coke,* she thought. *When he goes after something, he won't stop until he gets it.*

It wasn't until one evening toward the end of the summer when he was preparing to go to Virginia Tech on a full scholarship that Idella finally asked him, "William, I know that years ago you really changed when Mr. Estrada was your substitute teacher, and I suppose it was because you liked him. However, I was truly concerned that you would go back to your old ways when you went into fifth grade. I am glad you didn't, but can you tell me why?"

William, who towered over his grandmother at six feet after a late senior year growth spurt, reached out and gently took her into his muscular arms. "You, of all people, influenced me the most," he began. "Of course,

Mr. Estrada had something to do with it. His passion for what was going on in the rest of the world made me realize that there is more to living on this planet than just playing games with my friends. No one else in the class seemed to share my enthusiasm, but that didn't matter to me. I just wanted to learn as much as I could while I was still in his class."

He stopped for a second as if contemplating what to say next. Then he held Idella out at arm's length and looked into her gentle eyes. "If you want to know the truth, I worried in kind of the opposite direction, Grammy. I suddenly realized what I had done—finally getting good grades and all—which meant that you knew, like Mr. Estrada did, that I could do the work. If I went back to my old habits, you would be disappointed.

"I guess you could say I overplayed my hand and had to keep playing the game from then on. I had proven to myself that I could do the work, even if I didn't find it interesting. So I started fifth grade with a new attitude and the rest is history. Funny, once I made up my mind, I never thought about it again until you just mentioned it. I guess I found out that learning can be fun."

"Now it's on to Virginia Tech. I am so proud of you, William." Idella gave him a warm hug. "Your mother and father would be beaming with pride if they were here. The saddest day in my life turned out to be the beginning of the best 13 years anyone could ever ask for. I'll miss you, but it's time to let you go. Just promise that you will keep in touch with me, and that you will go to church."

"Graaaammmy!" William faked a whine. "I'm grown up now and don't need to go to church. You know, once a Christian, always a Christian."

"William J. Brantley, I know you're kidding, but you still have a lot to learn about having your own personal relationship with God. Just going to Sunday services is not enough. There still is a part that is missing, and I can't give it to you. When it fits into place, you will know it. It's no big secret, and I can talk until I am blue in the face, but until you have it, you will never know how precious it is." She stood on her tiptoes and kissed him on the cheek. "Now is there anything else you need? I don't want to wait until the last minute to get you packed."

Chapter 2

College Days

*V*irginia Tech! What a beautiful campus! William thought as he walked across the quad the third week of his freshman year. *If God is really here, I can't see Him. I still haven't found Grammy's secret. She said I would know it when it happens, but it certainly hasn't happened in Religion 101 although Professor Mickey Dugan sure makes the class come alive.* He snickered as his thoughts continued, *They used to joke in high school that Latin was dead and religion was not far behind. Well, someone should tell that to Professor Dugan. I have never seen anyone so passionate about God, anyone other than Grammy.*

"Hey, BB!" A familiar voice broke his concentration. "Wait up."

William turned around and walked backwards as LC Cunningham rushed toward him. "Sorry, LC, I just can't get used to this nickname business. My grandmother hated them and always insisted on using proper names." He shifted his backpack to the other arm and hefted it onto his left shoulder. "She claimed a person was given a name on their birth certificate, and that is what their parents intended them to be called."

"No insult intended, BB, but your grandmother sounds pretty old-fashioned," LC retorted.

"Oh, to the contrary, my friend, she's pretty hip for someone in her sixties. She has her quirks, all right, but who doesn't? She loves to read murder mysteries and gets a kick out of seeing the latest spy movies. Her taste in music does leave a little to be desired—but old-fashioned—nothing could be farther from the truth."

"I'd like to meet her someday," LC said. "From what you've told me, she sounds like a lot of fun. Where are you headed?

"Process Engineering. It's interesting stuff," William said.

BB and LC were assigned as roommates in Philo Hall, a low, two-story dorm on the west side of the campus. Their second floor room overlooked a sloping lawn that ended at the willow trees lining Tymoctee Creek. It was nice waking up to that scene on a colorful fall day, especially when they studied late the night before.

LC, the second of three children from a prominent black family in Richmond, had come to Virginia Tech with hopes of getting a football scholarship. He was practicing with the team this season as a walk-on. LC didn't put in much time with the books. William swore that his friend had a photographic memory. While William faithfully studied his class notes, LC mainly read novels, although he always managed to keep up with the assigned class reading too. LC's definition of studying was to pull out his notes and read through them usually an hour or two before a test. To William's surprise he consistently earned good grades. William figured LC's study habits would catch up with him later when the course work became more difficult, but they never did.

As they headed in opposite directions toward their classes, LC said, "See you at supper, BB."

William shrugged and nodded as he thought, *Don't let Grammy hear you call me that.* "Guess so. Do you have practice this afternoon?"

"Yeah. Even though we won big last time, Coach said we can never have enough practice." William would like to have been able to play football, but since he had worked during high school to help Grammy make ends meet, he had had no time to make that kind of commitment. He also knew that he would never be good enough to earn a sports scholarship. Even though there was an insurance settlement from his parents' car accident, Grammy insisted on using as little as possible of that money for day to day expenses so that William would have enough left to go to college. William had agreed and when he turned 16, he set out to earn extra money in various ways in case he did not receive an academic scholarship.

He watched as LC lumbered toward Evans Hall. BB thought, *He hasn't earned a scholarship yet, but I can see him playing next year. Then he might move into the sports dorm; I guess I'd miss him if he did.*

After Process Engineering class, William moved on to Professor Dugan's Religion 101. The Professor was on a roll. He was talking about great leaders in biblical history who turned people to God by pointing out that they were spiritually dry. These leaders told the people they had to give up their sinful ways of living or face God's consequences. William snickered loud enough for the professor to hear when he used one of Grammy's favorite sayings.

"And Moses brought them kicking and screaming back to God to atone for their sins." He looked at William. "Do you find this amusing, Mr. Brantley?"

"Not the atonement for sins, Professor. But the way you said it reminded me of someone else who loves to use that phrase until wayward people finally see things her way."

The professor smiled and nodded in acknowledgement, "I would like to meet her some day. Now back to the lesson." He paused to make sure he picked up where he left off. "From Moses to Nehemiah we see how great leaders encouraged repentance in biblical history, turning great numbers of people back to God. Don't you find it interesting that these were God's chosen people, and yet He had to keep reminding them about it through various leaders who took action and were not afraid to make His desires known? Throughout history, however, they still turned their backs on Him. To paraphrase Moses, 'How stiff-necked can a people be?'"

The professor continued, "Look at the miracles He performed in their days. For instance, God, through Moses, parted the waters of the Red Sea. Now walking between two walls of water would certainly get my attention! But it was not long afterwards when the Israelites began to worship false Gods and He had to get their attention again. I could go on and on talking about great leaders in the Bible, and we will discuss them as the semester progresses, but I have given you a list that I consider to be some of the greatest. I want you to pick out just one leader, use one of the Bible verses I have given you, and write a two-page paper on why you chose this particular person and portion of scripture. The papers are due one week from today. Class dismissed."

William scanned the sheet with the title "Great Leaders in the Bible" as he walked back to the dorm. Without hesitation he picked Jehoshaphat along with the verses in 2 Chronicles 20 that describe when Jehoshaphat commanded the Israelites to trust in God alone to help them, and their discouragement turned to joy. *He's one of Grammy's favorite Bible leaders. She would be proud of me for picking him.*

Professor Dugan had pointed out the Israelites' tendencies to stray from God. William thought about this as he found a bench to sit on and read the verses assigned to him. He quickly saw that even with firsthand observance of the power of God, the Israelites once again found reason to idolize false gods.

In the story of Jehoshaphat, when the Israelites were faced with disaster and utter annihilation, God gave them an unusual battle plan. He told them to take their positions, stand still, and watch the glory of God gain victory on their behalf.

William thought, *Even with the thousands killed in one morning and their praise of God for saving them, it was not long before they went back to their old ways and turned their backs on Him. Professor Dugan was right. We humans do have short memories.*

William chuckled at this observation. An idea for his paper was taking shape. He took out a notepad and began to jot down his thoughts.

William loved campus life. He had become good friends with LC and shared a dorm room with him all four years. William and LC became close friends with JJ Walker who had a new roommate each year. JJ was pre-med and loved to hit the bars on the weekend in search of a pretty co-ed. William usually served as their designated driver, just in case LC and JJ over-imbibed.

LC was able to make arrangements to keep the same room and store their belongings locally so they did not have to haul them back and forth at the end of each year. They were alike in many aspects but differed in how they wanted to be involved in campus life. LC was more tuned into campus politics while William liked getting involved in various campus youth organizations. No matter how hard William tried, LC showed little or no interest in studying about God. He met the basic university curriculum requirements and "That's that," he would tell William whenever the subject was broached. BB thought it best to wait for the opportune time to nudge LC along, but the time never seemed to come.

———◆•◆•◆———

William worked at the campus library for three hours a day twice a week. He liked the work and enjoyed meeting those involved with Virginia Tech. Of course, it was not long before he knew many people on a first-name basis, professors, of course, excluded. Grammy raised William to respect his elders and those in authority, thus it was always, "Good morning, Professor Phelps." Never would he call them by their first name like many of his fellow students insisted on doing. *No, I have not yet earned that right. Possibly when I graduate* he would think, but when he finally graduated from Virginia Tech, he still hesitated to place himself on the same level as those who taught him and who had gained his utmost respect.

After two years at the university, William was fairly confident that he had seen most of the faces on campus, that is until that wonderful, fall Saturday morning when he was covering for a sick friend at the library's information desk. William watched dumbstruck as the most beautiful woman in the world (at least to him) walked across the terrazzo floors of Temple Hall toward him, her slim body shadowed by the sun. As she reached the desk, the books she held close to her slipped out of her hands. Before he realized what he was doing, William was kneeling next to her, helping to pick them up. As he handed them back, she pulled her shoulder length auburn hair away from her face. Her radiant smile melted his heart while a large lump formed in his throat.

"Thank you, ah..." she stared at his nametag, "William," she spoke softly.

The voice of an angel, he thought as he tried to regain his composure. "You're welcome," he struggled to answer, "it's my pleasure to help."

"Are you new around here?" William finally asked after collecting his wits. *She's so beautiful,* he thought.

Something on the left side of her sweater sparkled and caught his eye. *She's pinned!* he thought. *Of all the luck!* According to the "code of pinning," William could not even ask her out for a soda. *Nuts!*

"I'm Sarah Worthington," she stuck her hand out to shake his.

William slowly reached out and took her hand in his. *It's so soft and small,* he thought. Clicking the heels of his running shoes which made only a thud, he teasingly bowed, "William J. Brantley, at your service."

"Well, William J. Brantley, I'm not from Virginia Tech. I'm a sophomore at Butler and came for a long weekend to see my hometown friend, Leslie Watson. Maybe you know her?"

"So you're from Marietta?"

"You know her then."

"Absolutely. She sat next to me in Comparative Literature. Wow, that's a long trip!"

"That's what buses are made for, though I hitched a ride with some friends this time."

William nodded at the pin on her blouse. "I'm surprised your boyfriend would let you come this far alone."

"You could say that he's a little overprotective, but he knows where I am most of the time. Anyway, thanks for your help, William J. Brantley. I have to get back."

William was crestfallen. He was letting the woman of his dreams walk away because of some silly rule. "Sarah," he called after her, his courage growing.

"Yes," she turned to look at him.

"Enjoy your stay."

"I fully intend to. Do you work all day?"

"Not usually. I'm covering for someone this morning so I'll have to work my shift this afternoon until three."

"Well, don't work too hard. It was nice meeting you." She turned and walked toward the door.

"You too," he whispered.

That afternoon as he was leaving the library, a familiar voice called out behind him, "Hey, stranger."

He turned and much to his disbelief it was Sarah Worthington.

"I don't want you to think I'm stalking you, but I have to show you something. Maybe *not* show you something is a better term. Notice anything different from this morning?"

"Same clothes, same hairstyle, same smile," he wished he had stopped while he was ahead.

"You're silly, William J. Brantley," she teased as she pointed to her left shoulder. "Something's missing."

"You're not wearing your pin! What did you do, call and break it off?"

"Not exactly. I'll fill you in over a snack. How does that sound?"

"W-Wonderful," he stuttered.

Sarah and William sat in a corner table at Sebastiano's, a small Italian delicatessen just outside VT's campus. William was still in semi-shock that this gift from God was sitting across the table from him, munching on some fries and sipping a soda. *What did I do to deserve this?* he thought as she started to explain.

"That was my father's fraternity pin you saw this morning. I guess you could say that Dad was my pin-mate if you take it to extremes. William, I don't want to appear prideful or bold, but the reason that I wear the pin is to keep from getting hit on by guys that I have little or no interest in."

William pondered what she had just said. "I don't know whether to be flattered or disappointed. But why me?"

"I know what I want out of life, and one thing that I don't want is having to fight off hormonal guys who think that women are for nothing but their pleasure. In high school I got tired of guys pawing me all the time, especially those my mom and dad thought were a good match because they were friends with their parents. One traumatic night, my dad heard me crying in my bedroom after a horrible date. I told him what had happened, and he agreed with me that I did not have to put up with it. Thus, my father gave me his fraternity pin when I left for college." She reached in her purse and placed it on the table.

"His idea worked most of the time, not because of the pin, but I let it be known that my pin-mate was a defensive tackle who was six-foot four and weighed 260 pounds. No one ever caught on that I was describing my father," she smiled as he fingered the pin.

"Why me?" he asked again.

"It's those freckles and red hair—and—that charm.

Seriously, William, you didn't size me up like a lot of guys do. You were polite and offered to help. After that, I talked to Leslie, and she gave me the low down on one William J. Brantley. Is that good enough for now?"

"I can't honestly say that I didn't size you up, Sarah. I was struck by the way you walked and your smile—that's what did me in."

"Are you saying you're interested in me, William J. Brantley?"

"Does the interest go two ways?" he asked.

She smiled and nodded yes. "How about you?"

"Oh, does it really—I mean it really does," he blurted out.

"Where do we go from here?" she asked.

"How about a movie tonight?" he asked reaching for her hand.

"No horror flicks, I just don't understand what guys see in them."

"You just name it."

That night was the first of many dates over the next two years as Sarah and William became an item on both the Butler and VT campuses.

Chapter 3

A Fork in the Road

"Wake up, BB," William heard his name whispered close to his ear as he felt a hand shake his shoulder.

"Huh?" the sleep deprived college student mumbled.

"BB, it's Case," Bill Case, senior floor counselor for Philo Hall, said much louder this time. He had used his passkey to get in.

"What?" a confused William exclaimed.

"BB, there's been an accident."

"An accident! Sarah?" He was now wide awake and bolted upright in bed. He looked across the room to wake up LC and noticed he was not there.

"Where's LC? Is he dressed already?"

"No. LC was in the accident, so drop any concerns about Sarah. Look, all I know is that the State Police called the university and said a couple of students were in an accident over on Harper's Road, just below Miller's Dam. I know one is LC because he asked the police to call me, and I think, but I'm not sure, the other one is JJ."

26

William was out of bed and halfway out the room, still zipping up his pants and buckling his belt when he called back over his shoulder, "Which hospital did they take them to?"

"County Memorial...but hold on there, my friend, I'm coming with you."

When they arrived at the hospital, Bill Case's counselor status as a representative of the university was a big help in cutting through the red tape. They were finally able to meet with the head of the trauma department, Walter Barrett. Dr. Barrett, dressed in green hospital scrubs, took them into a small conference room.

He didn't beat around the bush. "Lawrence is in critical condition in the Intensive Care Unit. He suffered some pretty severe injuries. He's still in a coma, but we've been able to stop the bleeding. It's touch and go for the next few hours. His face is pretty cut up from the impact.

"But," he hesitated, "I'm sorry to have to tell you that Jamal died at the scene. There was nothing the paramedics could do."

This news hit William like a ton of bricks. "JJ—he's dead? No! That can't be! It must be someone else!"

"Case..." William cried out, his face white as a sheet, "They asked me to drive tonight because they were going out to celebrate finishing their mid-terms, but I said no because I was getting up early to go see Sarah."

"Now, don't go blaming yourself, BB," Case consoled his distraught friend. "They could have called you—or even me—if they felt they were not capable of driving. No, BB, don't lay this on yourself."

"But, Case, they asked me to go and I begged off, just so I could get a good night's sleep." BB turned to Dr. Barrett. "When can we see him?"

"Not for awhile, not until we've notified his family and they give permission. Please write down your names for me so that I will have them with me when I talk to them."

Bill Case grabbed a notepad off the conference table along with a pen and handed it to William whose hands were shaking so much that he handed the materials back to the counselor.

"I can't do it." he said, "Would you mind?"

Case took the pen and paper back and began to write. "Sure," he sympathetically replied. When he finished, he handed the pad to Dr. Barrett.

"I'll be back as soon as I can. You're welcome to wait here, if you like."

"Thank you, Doctor," the young men said in unison.

After about ten minutes, William finally said, "Bill, I've got to make a couple of calls. It's almost six. I know Grammy is just getting up. I'll call Sarah and tell her I'm not coming this weekend."

Case nodded his approval. "You be OK?"

"Just stunned out of my head. Case, I should have been there..." William said as he looked back over his shoulder in the doorway.

For the next 45 minutes William talked with Grammy and Sarah on the phone. Both of them expressed their concern for him, but the young man sloughed it off with the typical male macho phrase, "I'm fine. I can handle this."

Just a little before noon, William was surprised when Grammy, Sarah, Reverend Harrelson, and Sarah's parents whom he had never met, walked into the waiting room. He wasn't sure what to say to them, but he appreciated their support.

———◆•◆•◆———

For the next two weeks, BB rarely left LC's bedside after he found out what he had been dreading to hear—both young men's blood alcohol level had been extremely high at the time of the accident. He did attend JJ's funeral the following Wednesday where he apologized to JJ's family for not having driven the two guys that fateful night. Through their tears, Jamal's parents comforted William by telling him that Jamal had made the decision to drive despite his condition, but William would not listen.

He even shut out Grammy's and Sarah's consoling attempts, though they never gave up. During a phone call with Sarah one evening, Grammy encouraged her, "Just keep on doing what you have been doing. Eventually it will sink into his thick skull that he's not to blame. And don't you get down on yourself because he was coming to see you. Death is a part of life, Sarah. God is working in the midst of this difficult time. You have to believe that."

"I know, Grammy, but I have found out through experience that God's way is many times the hard way."

LC's football teammates took turns relieving William at times to let him return to the dorm to shower, shave, get a fresh change of clothes, and catch a few winks. He was not sleeping well, and when he did sleep, he had nightmares of the accident. His overactive conscience worked hard, convincing him that he was to blame for the accident. He never responded to Grammy's, Sarah's, or Case's counsel that LC and JJ were old enough and responsible enough to know that they should not have been driving that night.

BB's professors understood his situation and made sure that one of his friends brought his assignments to the hospital so he could complete his course work and still graduate with his class. Bill Case made arrangements for BB to take his exams in one of the conference rooms if Case was present to monitor.

BB did study, but his focus was on LC whose parents were in Malta on some sort of business trip and were having trouble scheduling a flight to get back due to an airlines strike. He read his textbooks out loud so that LC would hear his voice and not the sounds of the clicking and pulsating machines that were keeping him alive.

"I'm sure that you'll find this interesting," he said as he read about organic chemistry or quantum physics, things LC would never understand even if he were awake.

He still spent time apologizing to his comatose friend for not having gone with them that night. It was not long before BB accepted full blame for the accident. Grammy, Sarah, and most of those around him noticed the change. He became short and cryptic with everyone, but they seemed to understand what he was going through and accepted his mood swings. William was not handling the crisis well at all.

The second week after the accident, LC was still in a coma and not responding to treatment. BB felt a mixture of relief and dread that LC's parents were finally in the United States and winging their way from the west coast. Turning to the small radio on LC's nightstand, he flipped it on. The announcer said, "And next, the newest hit from The Apostles, 'God Is Always at Your Side.'"

If you walk away from God,
Always keep in mind,
In times of trouble
Our Lord and Savior's
Always at your side.
When He walked with you,
You saw two sets of footprints,
But when there is only one,
They're His prints as he carried you,
In troubled times,
He's always at your side.

BB's jaw dropped open as he felt something stir deep within him. He bolted from the room, bumping into a nurse. As he apologized for almost knocking her over, he asked, "Does this hospital have a chapel?"

"Of course. Second floor, past the nurses station on your right."

"Thank you!" he exclaimed as he headed for the stairwell.

31

BB slowly opened the door to the Dr. Thomas King Memorial Chapel, which proclaimed that it welcomed people of all faiths. It was small in comparison to a church, having only six rows of pews, but there was an altar and railing, a large cross, and a folding screen divider. As BB entered the room, he noticed a middle-aged man in a work uniform quietly straightening things in the back of the room.

He began to think about LC and JJ and how they had so much going for them in their lives. *They were almost ready to graduate! Why them?* In the midst of his thoughts, BB began to feel a little frustrated. He had come to the chapel for some private time and this guy was humming softly to himself as he headed up the aisle. He abruptly decided he wasn't going to find any comfort in the chapel and was about to leave when the man in the uniform stood next to him and spoke.

"Somethin' troublin' you, young man? Anythin' I can help ya with? Name's Mick, but everybody here just calls me Brother Mick." He spoke with a simple southern drawl as he turned and looked at BB with a kindly smile.

At first BB was about to brush aside the man's questions and leave, but suddenly he knew he couldn't hold his pain inside any longer.

"Is it that obvious, sir?" Throwing caution to the wind, BB began to unburden himself.

"You know, I promised my grandmother, who has taken care of me since my parents were killed in a car accident, that I would go to church every Sunday. I have not been very faithful to that pledge since I've been in college. I think my friend, LC, is lying in that bed upstairs because I have more or less walked away from the church. 'Course I'm still involved in some Christian activities on campus. I guess I thought that would take the place of going to church. And, my friend, JJ, he was killed—I just don't understand...."

The older man smiled. "Can't say as I know exactly what you're goin' through. But I would like ya to know that even if ya feel that you've turned your back on God, all ya have to do is turn around. It doesn't take much to get back into the fold. He's always there, listening to what's in ya heart. Don't ever lose sight of that."

BB sighed as he shook his head and said, "That's the second time I've heard that today." He described the song that caused him to seek out the chapel.

"Yeah, sometimes music speaks to my heart, too."

The man nodded toward the front altar and asked BB, "Would ya care to join me?"

He put his hand on BB's shoulder and walked with him to the front. At the railing, they both knelt down and BB dropped his face into his hands.

"Ya know, prayin's just like talkin' to a friend," the kindly custodian began. "I can guarantee ya God's fixin' to listen to ya. Keep in mind that He has a purpose for everythin' that happens in this world."

Kneeling there, BB didn't know where to start.

"Have faith and just start at the beginnin'. Tell God what's troublin' ya," the man encouraged.

As though an inner dam had broken, BB poured his heart out, sharing his thoughts and feelings about the nightmare that began when Bill Case woke him up. He didn't leave out a thing. He finished by confessing how selfish he had been when he refused to go out with his friends that fateful night and how, since then, he was cold and impatient with all his friends and family. BB began to sob as the custodian placed his hand on his shoulder to comfort him.

"Lord," BB prayed between sobs, "I've walked away from You, not knowing what I had. How can You ever forgive me? I don't deserve Your forgiveness. It's hard to understand, but I need to know You forgive me."

After a few minutes, the man said, "He's heard ya, all right. Rest assured, God understands."

William mumbled a thank you to the older man and started down the aisle. As he opened the chapel door, he looked at his watch. He was surprised that he had been in the chapel over an hour and began to panic, thinking no one was with LC during that time. BB raced back up to LC's floor, taking the stairs two at a time. As he rounded the corner of the nurses' station, he noticed Dr. Barrett standing next to LC's door.

"Is LC all right?" he gasped, short of breath from his quick dash up three flights of stairs.

"He's showing good signs of improvement. I was so encouraged by what I just saw that I took him off the respirator."

"That's great news!" BB shouted in relief.

Just then they heard a raspy voice call out, "Where am I and who's making all that racket out there?"

It was LC and he was awake! Rushing to his friend's side, William gave out a shout when he saw his friend weakly smiling up at him. The doctor rushed in right behind him and checked him out. Giving William the thumbs up, Dr. Barrett left them to catch up.

BB began to explain to his friend what had transpired over the last two weeks, answering LC's questions as best as he could. Not wanting to tire out his friend, BB told him he'd let him rest and headed toward the public phones. He called Grammy and Sarah and apologized for his recent poor behavior and asked for their forgiveness. William shared with them about his encounter with Brother Mick and his encouraging words. "I know God's with us and that He's working through all of this. We just have to trust Him."

Both Grammy and Sarah were relieved that William had finally been returned to them. During the next few weeks both William and Sarah worked hard to catch up on what they had missed in their classes.

Chapter 4

A New Beginning

One hot and humid evening near the end of their senior year, Sarah sat next to William in a tent about the size of a small one used in the circus. Huge circulating fans, strategically placed throughout the tent, kept the air moving just enough so that the large audience could tolerate the heat.

They were both excited because they had never experienced such an event. A huge banner proclaiming Tony Hall Ministries dangled from support ropes over the center stage. The couple recognized the familiar pop rock Christian songs that blared over the sound system from the Campus Crusade activities they had attended on both campuses. During the two years they had been dating, they had become very active in the Campus Crusade for Christ organization. In fact William took Sarah to a meeting on their second date and could not sleep that night because he worried that she might think he was odd. When he called her the next week, he found his worries were in vain because she had just joined the crusade organization on her campus. Within a few months, they each assumed a leadership role in their respective group.

William leaned over to Sarah, "It looks like we're going to have evangelism in the round," he said as he nudged her with his elbow. Then he joked, "When will they bring in the clowns?"

"Now you promised to be serious, BB." It had been her idea to attend. She had always wanted to go to a revival meeting just to see what they were like. Hall's placards had appeared one Monday evening announcing the meeting the following Friday. Since it was being held only a ten-minute walk from the Butler campus, they went. The bleachers were so crowded the young couple stood at the front, scanning the rows and not seeing any empty seats. In the front row, an older Hispanic couple, who introduced themselves as Carlos and Maria, took pity on them and squeezed them in. During the service, Carlos became so entranced in Hall's message that he actually slid off his seat and squatted in front of them, making more room. Later, after Sarah had thanked him for his kind gesture, the migrant worker said he labored like that all day, usually in the hot sun, and was not uncomfortable. "Think nothing of it, Senorita," he said. "Mi Dios brought us all here for a reason, and I actually felt more humbled before Him sitting on the ground."

After several musical numbers by a local group of singers, Tony Hall took the stage with little introduction. He was a bear of a man, dressed in black slacks and white shirt with his sleeves already rolled up to his elbows. During the entire service, he carried a well-worn

Bible, its black cover worn around the edges from constant use, his index finger inserted amongst the pages so he could easily find the proper supportive verse when needed.

BB listened intently as Hall spoke about the Holy Spirit and how He made a powerful difference in his life and could do the same for them as well if only they accepted Jesus Christ into their lives as their Lord and Savior. William had heard this message preached many times over the years by various preachers and religious instructors, but never in the manner he witnessed this evening. The evangelist's vibrant energy was contagious, as people, caught up in the moment, jumped to their feet praising God.

He heard Carlos say to his wife in Spanish, *"Su mensaje es para ambos. ¿Qué piensas tú?"*

She responded "Yes, my husband, his message is for both of us. We must listen closely. No?"

"Si," he said as he nodded his head in agreement.

William heard the couple speaking back and forth in a mixture of English and Spanish, but because he could not speak their language, he could not understand all of it. Along with Sarah, he was impressed with their bilingual abilities. BB leaned over to her and whispered, "One thing I want to do if I ever get the chance is to learn another language and be able to really communicate well with it."

As Hall kept his torrid pace, reaching crescendo after crescendo in his sermon, William began to experience a growing sense of conviction. Hall seemed to be working his utmost to express the love and fear of God to those

38

shouting His praise. William remembered the loneliness and helplessness he had felt when LC was laying critically injured. He felt that at last he understood the depth of God's love for him. William knew that God was calling him personally.

When the preacher issued the invitation to come and "accept Jesus Christ as your Lord and Savior," William quickly made his decision. Responding to the call of a loving God, the Virginia Tech senior followed Carlos and his wife who walked forward toward Hall. BB felt Sarah's hand reach out for his as he moved to make what he was sure was the most important decision he would ever make in his life. Sarah did not hesitate, and William was glad that she was with him, though this was so out of character for both of them. They were rational people and only made practical decisions. Yet, here they were, standing with this large crowd at the foot of Hall's stage, professing for the world to see that they accepted Jesus Christ as their personal Lord and Savior.

The young couple looked into each other's tear-filled eyes, both realizing the importance of the moment. William grasped Sarah's hand tightly as he raised them both into the air. Together they declared, "Come into my heart and my life, Lord Jesus. Forgive me of my sins and be my God." At that moment they both knew that Jesus had answered their simple prayer.

As they were passing in front of Tony Hall, who was speaking with the new believers, Hall reached out and placed his hand on William's head and prayed for him. William looked into Hall's eyes and heard the preacher's prayer followed by, "I would like to see you in my trailer after the service, young man. Please come." William was confused but nodded his head that he would be there.

When they had resumed their places, Sarah exclaimed, "What a wonderful feeling to know that we both came to Jesus at the same time. BB, that means a great deal to me." She took his hands into hers as they stared into each other's eyes, not knowing what to say.

"How much?" he finally asked. "Enough..." his voiced trailed off.

"Enough what?" she asked. She cocked her head to one side giving him an inquisitive look as she swung their hands to and fro between them.

"Enough to realize that—that—you should—Sarah.... Aw nuts, this is not how I planned it, but tonight it means more than ever to me. I wanted just the right moment and mood...will you marry me?" he finally blurted out.

"What's wrong with accepting Christ in one breath alongside the man I love and saying yes to his marriage proposal with the other? What better moment could I ask for?"

"You mean you'll marry me?"

She answered, "Just to make it official, YES!"

"You mean we're engaged?"

"Yes, but it's not official until you kiss me."

William swept her into his arms and kissed her with a love and passion saved only for those truly in love and committed to one other.

Fifteen minutes later, Sarah and William were standing in front of an old Airstream trailer behind the huge meeting tent. William politely knocked and the door opened immediately. They were welcomed inside by a lively, petite woman, her hair pulled tightly back into a pony tail. She gestured toward a couch at one end of the room. "Please be seated. My husband will be out in a moment. He's changing into something more comfortable."

Dressed in a denim shirt and blue jeans, Tony Hall entered through a sliding door on the other side of the small kitchen. William and Sarah politely rose from their seats. "I am Tony Hall. And you are...?" he said reaching out to shake William's hand.

"William J. Brantley. BB to my friends."

Before turning and looking at Sarah, Hall said, "I hope to someday call you BB, then. And this is...?"

"Sarah Worthington," William introduced her.

As she reached out to shake Hall's hand he said, "Your bride to be."

Sarah blushed and took her place on the sofa next to William.

Tony smiled as he sat down in a large comfortable chair directly in front of the newly engaged couple. William's first impression was that Tony was not as large as he looked on the stage during the meeting. The evangelist was still profusely perspiring. He motioned again to the couch. "May we offer you something cold to drink?" he asked as they were taking their seats.

"Water would be fine." Sarah responded first, and looking over at BB, added, "for both of us."

Mrs. Hall went to the refrigerator and opened the door while Reverend Hall mopped his face with a large white towel wrapped around his neck.

"Obviously you have a lot of questions for me. But let me answer them before you have to ask. Then if I have missed anything, you can pursue what's left."

After Mrs. Hall served the ice water, she joined them in a chair next to her husband.

"I bet you're wondering why I asked to talk to you, William."

"Well, yes, I guess that's my first question," William responded.

"It's hard for me to say what prompted me." Tony shrugged his shoulders. "From backstage I always watch as people enter the tent to see the type of individuals I will be preaching to. Usually people your age come for a lark and mock what I do. No insult intended." He leaned forward in his chair, the towel still draped around his neck. He took one end and wiped the perspiration from his forehead once again. His wife rose to turn the fan more directly on him, and he smiled appreciatively at her.

"I saw how you responded gratefully when the Hispanic couple offered to squeeze you in. Many young people would not appreciate their sacrifice. And Sarah and you both sat and listened intently as I spoke. It is hard to explain fully, except that I always pray that the Lord will send me young people who want to learn more about Him. The younger someone is that I can lead to Christ, the better are the possibilities that he or she will have a significant impact for Christ, not only on their own generation but on future generations as well. That is what I wanted to say to you. Take your relationship with God as far as you can."

He paused. "I received similar advice not long after I arrived in America. My family was Russian Catholic and they wanted me to be a priest, thus I ended up in a seminary in upper New Jersey. My Russian name was too hard for Americans to pronounce, so like many of our Hollywood actors, I changed my name to something simpler, Tony Hall. Actually, I did not want to become a priest, though from the depths of my soul I wanted to preach the word of Jesus Christ. Then I had an unusual encounter during my second year in seminary." He paused and took a large drink of water.

"An elderly missionary who had spent her entire adult life rescuing and caring for orphaned children in China made a visit to the United States and stayed for two nights at our seminary. Early one morning during her stay, I could not sleep and found myself in a small seminary chapel, kneeling at the front altar, praying, asking God what to do. I heard a stirring behind me only to find her curled up, asleep on the front pew with her hands as her pillow. She looked so frail. All of her belongings were packed in a box tied with rope." He stopped, pondering the memorable experience.

"I was struck by what I saw—her sleeping on the hard wooden pew at peace as if she were on a comfortable bed. She must have sensed my presence because soon she sat up and started talking to me. For over an hour we discussed the conflict in my heart—my wanting to preach the word of Jesus yet not wanting to become a priest. 'Tony,' she said, 'you are a very troubled young man. God wants you to follow your heart and to do His bidding, not that of other people. Many times other people mean well, but do not know God's direction for our lives.'"

"We sat up until the wee hours of the morning putting together my options." Hall laughed. "Tonight, as I saw you sitting there, I witnessed what that dear lady must have seen in me—a young man destined to deliver God's word in unexpected ways. Now don't get me wrong, you don't have to be a preacher to do that. You can deliver it from whatever vocation you choose. All I am asking is to consider that God has a special purpose for you."

"You hit the nail on the head, Mr. Hall," BB said as he straightened up on the couch. "In the meeting I decided I wanted to serve God the rest of my life, but I also have always felt like I was supposed to have my own business some day. I'm really confused, just like you were. What am I supposed to do?" William asked.

"That I cannot tell you, my friend, but you will know. I can only tell you that this dear lady advised me to finish my studies first, and that God would show me what, where, and when I was to do my special work on His behalf. 'Just pray and listen.' That was her most profound advice. Not long after I graduated from seminary, God unmistakably arranged circumstances so that I knew He called me to do this." He pointed outside to where they were tearing down the tent in preparation for moving on to the next city. "When I see them doing that it reminds me of the Apostle Paul, who was a tentmaker by trade. What awesome footsteps to follow in!"

He reached in his shirt pocket, pulled out a crinkled business card, and handed it to William. "I am at your service if you ever need me. You can leave a message at this number and rest assured, William, I will return your call. After our brief discussion, I would like to talk to you more. Maybe I could at least be a sounding board for you and actually become a close enough friend to call you BB."

Before they left, William finally asked him the question that he'd been anxious to pose. "I have to ask you—how did you know that Sarah and I became...?

"Engaged tonight?" Tony finished his sentence. His roaring laughter filled the small confines of the trailer. "The radiant look on her face. I've only seen that a few times in my life, the first being when I proposed to Elena and she accepted." He looked over at his smiling wife. "That, my friends, was the easiest call of the evening."

He looked at a blushing Sarah. "God bless you both, and please, William, keep in touch." He stood and asked, "Would you like to close our time together in prayer with me?"

———

It was just a little before midnight when Idella's bedside phone rang. Still half asleep she answered, "Hello."

"Will you accept a collect call from a William Brantley?" the operator asked.

Wide awake at the mention of her grandson's name, "Yes! William, are you all right?"

"I'm fine, Grammy, the best I have ever been in my entire life," he said in an excited voice. "I'm calling from Sarah's dorm, so I don't have much time before they kick me out. I found out the secret. All I had to do was open my heart to Jesus and truly accept Him as my Lord and Savior—that happened tonight, Grammy. That happened tonight for Sarah and me. Even working with the Campus Crusades, I found myself mouthing the words, but Sarah and I went to a tent evangelism meeting tonight and..."

William went on to explain what they had experienced, culminating with the meeting with Pastor Tony Hall and his wife. "Oh, by the way, Sarah's agreed to marry me, that is if her father will let her."

"Still wearing his pin, is she? William, all kidding aside, I could not be happier for you both! Sarah is a very special girl, and I always knew that you would find the secret of Christ, though it's not much of a secret at all, is it? Once you make that decision, He's always with you. Your grandfather, even with all his problems, always said, 'No matter how far you stray from Christ, all you have to do is turn to Him. He's always there.' I used to remind him to turn and look all the time." She paused. "William, I have always been proud of you, and I don't want this to sound like a doting grandmother. But I have been persistent in saying, probably to the annoyance of all my friends, that you are anointed for something great and now God has started you down His narrow road." She paused and cleared her throat. "When are you coming home? But first, let me talk to my future granddaughter-in-law."

Over the final few weeks of Sarah's and William's undergraduate years, Idella and Sarah quickly became very close; their only bone of contention being that Sarah loved to call her fiance BB. She understood Grammy's penchant for using proper names and strived to refer to him as William in front of her, with only a few slips that caused a raised brow. On the other hand, Grammy thought she was letting Sarah's little improprieties go unnoticed, never realizing that her facial expressions always betrayed her.

Except when he had to work at the library, William made the trek from Virginia Tech to Butler every weekend until they graduated. On several occasions, Idella and Sarah shared their concerns that William's '67 Dodge would give out and leave him stranded somewhere in a desolate part of Virginia. But the young suitor was determined that they were going to be together and would not listen to their arguments. To William, sleep deprivation was the larger danger; when he grew sleepy, he would pull off to the side of the road and catch a few winks. Somehow, he developed the knack of being able to sleep for ten minutes, wake up refreshed, and continue his journey. This gift would serve him well in his later business years.

During their weekly visits, the young couple started to plan the next few years of their lives. They would be married in a small ceremony on the Butler campus two days after Sarah graduated, the service to be performed by Tony Hall. After a short honeymoon, William planned to work for the Fuller and Sons Manufacturing Company as he had every summer during his undergraduate years.

He loved working on the floor, learning each step of the manufacturing process.

William was fortunate to receive a full scholarship for the MBA program at Harvard Business School. Earl Fuller called BB in his office the last day before he left for Harvard.

"William," the CEO said, "I know you are going on to business school, and I would like you to come back next summer to serve an internship in the administrative offices. I think you know enough about how the wonderful people on the floor make the guts of this operation work. I think it is time for you to learn how the business end functions. Of course, you will have to start at the bottom again, but I think it is important that you learn it all. What do you think?"

Without hesitation BB replied, "I would be honored, Mr. Fuller. You just tell me where and when to report."

"Fine," the CEO replied, "just call me two weeks before the school year ends and we'll discuss what you will be doing. I'll put it on my calendar to expect your call."

Chapter 5

Unexpected Blessing

While he was pursuing his MBA, the plan was for Sarah to find work as a teacher to help support them. Sarah and William did not want to touch any of the remaining money from the insurance settlement after his parents' accident. They hoped to use it to start a small business once William graduated and had worked in the business world for a few years. They planned to begin a family as soon as William found employment as a design engineer and then to "live happily ever after."

In June, William graduated summa cum laude from Virginia Tech. Idella, along with Sarah and her parents, sat proudly as William delivered a three-minute speech on his years at VT and how thankful he was to his professors for the wonderful education he had received. He told his fellow graduates, "This is one of the most exciting and happiest days of my life. It actually ranks third, the second happiest being the day Sarah Worthington accepted my marriage proposal. But the most important day of my life was when I came to know Jesus as my personal Savior."

As his words tumbled from the loudspeakers, tears began to trickle down Idella's cheeks. Before wiping her own eyes, Sarah offered Idella a tissue. When a beaming William, smiling from ear to ear, marched by during the recessional, Sarah's family discovered they all needed a tissue, and a proud Sarah gladly obliged.

——◆·◆·◆——

While attending Harvard, William missed the close knit Christian community of Campus Crusade for Christ at Virginia Tech. He felt isolated from his classmates because most of them focused on the ultimate goal of success, which they determined solely by the amount of money and prestige they could garner in the business world.

Of course BB wanted to be successful, but he was convinced that he needed more than money and prestige to be recognized as successful. No matter how corny it sounded to some of his fellow students, William wanted to give back and share his achievements with the rest of the world. Although most of his classmates and professors found little room in their world for Christ, BB was determined not to let their attitudes undermine his commitment.

William and Sarah found strength in each other's faith along with support from many calls to Tony, Grammy, and Sarah's parents. They lived in a small, one-bedroom apartment a few blocks from the university and were members of a small church on the edge of Boston, a few blocks from the Charles River campus. The newlyweds eventually joined a small Sunday school class, which provided them with needed friendship and support.

There were no teaching positions available for Sarah, so she set about transforming their cramped quarters into a special place. Her daily scouring of the help wanted sections began with a short prayer, but all she could find were waitress positions. She finally began to serve tables at a small deli around the corner. The pay wasn't much, but on occasion they let her take food home, which helped save money and gave Sarah the feeling that she was making a contribution. The couple treated these meals as romantic special dates, eating by candlelight at their small kitchen table with soft music playing in the background.

Sarah liked all the people she worked with at the deli. Most of them worked other jobs too, but the deli gave them a little money for a few extras in their lives. "I wouldn't call it a family affair," she once told William, "but we care about each other's problems."

After six months of waiting tables, Sarah noticed that at times, she became nauseous at the smell of certain foods. Other times, she felt light-headed. She thought she was fighting the flu, but when the symptoms persisted, she confided in Casey, one of the other waitresses.

"Girl, you're pregnant," Casey simply said.

Those three words cut like a knife. "I can't be," Sarah blurted out, "we've always used..."

"Protection," Casey finished her pronouncement. "Honey, get with the real world!" She rolled her eyes as she continued, "With the pill being only 98 percent effective, it means that two percent of women still become pregnant. I don't mean to be so blunt, but you'd better take one of them home pregnancy tests. Then you'll know for sure."

During a break Sarah went to the closest drugstore and purchased a pregnancy test. The deli was abuzz at the possibility of Sarah's unexpected news. When she returned, business came to a standstill while all the deli staff watched for her to emerge from the restroom.

Looking around at all their faces, she said one word, "Positive," and slouched against the door, a grim look on her face. Her actions told the story; getting pregnant right now was not part of their plan.

Casey walked over to her and gave her a big hug. "I know how it feels, honey," she comforted as Sarah started to cry. "All them plans you been makin', all gone up in smoke. It's just not right."

Sarah continued to cry. "BB and I had our lives all planned out and..." she looked down at her belly as she sniffled, "this little guy is too early."

Casey had worked part time at the deli almost five years while also a bank teller at a local savings and loan. She was determined to put her husband through med school so she understood Sarah's predicament. "You got insurance?" she asked Sarah.

"Oh, that's the least of my worries. BB took out health insurance at the university for the both of us. It's just…how will I ever tell him? We're on a really tight budget and this could put us over the edge."

"You know him better than me, but if he's half the man you say he is, he's gonna be one happy papa-to-be." She gave Sarah another gentle squeeze. "Now, do you think we can get some work done around here?"

Throughout the day, Sarah practiced how she was going to tell William. She definitely decided not to say she was sorry. After all, she was on the pill. No, she was going to tell him straightforward, knowing that was how he would want to hear it.

After dinner and before BB sat down at the kitchen table to study, Sarah told him the news.

"But—but you're on the pill."

"I'm sorry," she blurted as she thought, *Oh no, I wasn't going to say that.*

William could not believe what he was hearing and stared at her in shock that quickly turned to concern for her. "Please don't say you're sorry, Sarah. Please. I'm not blaming you. It took both of us and maybe a little divine intervention, you know, for this to happen."

"But all our plans, our dreams…" she said, "this could change them all."

"Maybe, maybe not. This is probably God's way of saying that we should be making our plans for Him and not us. As Grammy and your father would say, 'He's in control and He will see us through.' Let's give thanks to God for such a wonderful blessing." He placed his arms around her, pulled her close, and said a short prayer of thanksgiving.

Sitting down next to her on the sofa, he said, "I can

work weekends to help make ends meet. Just a few hours should help cover the loss of your wages. You are going to quit, aren't you?"

"Once I've seen a doctor, we can make that decision together. Work weekends if you need to, but I don't want you to quit your studies. With God's help, we can do this, the four of us, which includes our little gift," she smiled as she looked at his face. "You're okay with this. I can see the twinkle in your eyes."

"You bet I'm proud. What man wouldn't be? Having a child with the woman he loves, well it just doesn't get any better!" He leaned down and kissed her passionately.

"You'd better cut that out, Buster. That's what got us into this situation to begin with!"

"Too late, Love. You can't get any less pregnant." He swept her up in his arms and carried her toward the bedroom.

"What about your studies?"

"They can wait for one night."

Sarah wrapped her arms tightly around his neck. *Boy was Casey ever right—he is the man I told her he was.*

Two weeks before William's graduation, Keily Sarah Brantley was born. As they looked at the cherubic munchkin cradled safely in her mother's arms, Sarah remembered William sharing his fear of becoming a father. "But, Sarah, I've never held a baby before. What if she wiggles? I'm afraid I'll drop her."

"Look, silly," she remembered chiding him, "billions of men have handled babies without any prior experience. What makes you think you're any different?"

"Here," she nodded toward Keily, "it's time for a test run." She gently placed the infant into the green gowned arms of her father.

"Since you told me you were pregnant, I have prayed for the moment when I could hold our baby in my arms. Billions of men have done this, you know," he proudly reminded her as he looked down at Sarah and, while firmly holding Keily, kissed his wife. "Thank you for giving me this perfect gift."

"See, like I told you, there's nothing to holding a baby. But you were right, BB," she nodded toward the baby in his arms. "Having a baby right now is only a little bump in the road, but what a precious bump. I am so proud of you. Even though you worked weekends to help, in two weeks you're still graduating at the top of your class!" Sarah patted the bed beside her.

William gingerly handed Keily back to her before he sat down. He gently hugged them both and said, "All that matters to me at the moment are my two precious gifts from God sitting right here."

Chapter 6

The Business World

Mr. Fuller was a man of his word. For the two summers between William's years at Harvard, Mr. Fuller employed him in the administrative offices of Fuller and Sons, fulfilling the promise the CEO had made to him. In the beginning William was the office "gofer," performing any menial task that needed to be done. No matter how small or large the job, William completed it to their highest expectations, earning the respect of everyone in the office. They considered his work ethic and services so valuable they asked him if he would consider coming in during school breaks as well.

William liked working for the Fullers, and especially appreciated how they treated those who worked for them. They showed the utmost respect for everyone, no matter what their position. William admired how at least once a week they each left their offices and went to the manufacturing floor. These trips were not to check up on the quality of work, but to let the employees know that the Fullers were interested in them as individuals and did not view them as a machine putting parts together. They addressed their workers by their first names, and even knew their wives' and children's names, as well as some of their grandchildren's. The Fullers believed in helping their business family deal with their personal problems.

Early one morning during the second summer, Earl Fuller called William into his office.

"William, we are glad to have you working for us. You are a definite asset to our company, and I would like you to consider staying with us after you graduate, that is until you get your feet on the ground and want to pursue something on a larger scale. We can use a good design man like you, but from what I have seen, we can also use your business expertise." He placed a hand on William's shoulder as he winked, "Won't hurt to have our company profile show that we have a Harvard MBA working with us either."

Mr. Fuller let out a hearty laugh. "In all seriousness, BB, my sons and I see a lot of business potential in you and will do what we can to get you started. If you stick with us for two to three years after you graduate and let us pick your brain, we guarantee that we will help you make your next move, whatever you decide it to be. You don't have to answer me now, but just consider it, will you?"

That night at home while holding Keily in his lap, he told Sarah about his meeting with Mr. Fuller. "And Honey, just when you think you know all about a man,

Mr. Fuller, in all sincerity looked me straight in the eye and asked if I would mind praying with him about his offer. Of course, I told him yes. I know the Fuller family to be people of faith, but to pray in a business office, boy that takes guts in today's world. I have to say that moment was very special."

"I thought most businesses left their spirituality at the door," Sarah responded. "What happened next?"

"Sarah," William began, "after he placed his hand on my shoulder, he said the most wonderful prayer about you, Keily, and me. He just asked God's blessing on us and our future. It gave me goose bumps. I have heard him open many of our business meetings with prayer but nothing as eloquent as he prayed for me—or should I say, us."

"And then?"

"He motioned for me to sit down and said to never forget who brought us to where we are in the workplace. 'God has watched over us,' he said. 'We Fullers believe that without God's intervention we would not have the privilege to serve those who work for us. So we treat them the way He wants us to treat them. We never force prayer on them, but are never hesitant or afraid to ask someone experiencing problems at home if we can pray with them or for them. I have yet to have someone turn me down. William, we never hesitate to ask for God's advice on business decisions either. You just file that away for when you need it.'

"He winked at me and told me to think his offer over. It's been on my mind all day. I called Pastor Harrelson about what had happened. He just laughed and said that was Earl Fuller. 'He certainly tries to practice what I preach. William, I have known you for almost your entire life, and you can learn a lot from Earl Fuller. I'm going to give you a hypothetical for your future business, whatever it may be. Let's say, you now own your own business. Next, you have an employee who has two boys with a degenerative muscular disease requiring extra medical attention, which means, of course, more money is needed to take care of them. The company health insurance covers 80 percent of those needs, but the family is struggling to make ends meet because they have to pay their share. The person in question is a proud man; few people are aware of their misfortune. One of your employees confides in you about this unfortunate situation. What would you do?'

"I told him that I couldn't say for sure what I would do to help, but I certainly would find a way. I think, because of office politics, it would be difficult to pay him more than others in similar positions and it would not make business sense, but I would find a way.

"Pastor Harrelson then explained that such a family really exists. He knows a man who found out how much the medical bills cost for those two boys and makes sure the family receives the cash out of his own pocket. He said he's known that particular man to get out of bed at three in the morning to slide an envelope full of money under their front door. Then Pastor shared, 'Or he just gives the money to me and I act as the middleman, so to speak. It's just the way he is. So maybe you can learn something from that, William.'

"Sarah, I want to be like that man; I want to help, but I would never want people to know what I was doing."

"Silly man, you already are like that and don't you forget it."

———◆•◆•◆———

"BB, it's time," Sarah nudged William gently in his side.

"Time!" the expectant father shouted as he sat up at attention.

"Better call the Masters and tell them that you are bringing Keily over."

In the maternity suite William paced nervously as the nurses prepped Sarah for delivery.

A little over a year had passed since he had started as a design engineer with Fuller. He liked his work and saw the potential for moving up the corporate ladder in the company. He enjoyed being able to follow the Fullers when they walked the manufacturing floor and conversed with those workers who had taught him so much. He gained knowledge from the many design suggestions from those conversations, but he always let those who gave him ideas receive the credit for them. William soon learned that a Harvard degree does not make you an expert all the time. He recognized his gift for utilizing the talents of others to create a better product. In fact, he received permission from Earl Fuller to start a recognition program for those employees whose suggestions helped the company move forward.

But today all his attention was focused on Sarah and the birth of their child. He watched as the baby was delivered and heard its first cry. Within minutes, Sarah held the newborn in her arms and said, "Kevin, I want you to meet your father, William J. Brantley, or BB as I call him, or according to your sister, Keily, Boo Boo." She smiled as she looked from Kevin to his father. "He's number two."

"And number three is on its way!" a surprised Dr. James Wilson said.

"What?" Sarah and BB cried in unison.

"You have twins. I'm afraid you have a little more work to do, right now, young lady."

"How can that be?" Sarah asked.

A nurse took Kevin from Sarah and placed him in a bassinet as Dr. James explained that sometimes twins' heartbeats mask each other.

After five minutes of coaching, Dr. Wilson held up the second squalling infant and said, "It's another boy. What are you going to call him?"

As they placed the baby into a shocked Sarah's arms, she cried out, "I don't know...I don't know....We never expected twins!"

"Well, name him after me, James," the doctor suggested.

Sarah looked up at BB who was still stunned by this unexpected blessing.

"How does, James, meet your daddy and your brother, Kevin, sound?"

"Sounds like heaven to me," Dr. Wilson said.

BB, smiling from ear to ear, nodded his approval.

———◆◆◆◆———

The next three years were a blur for the Brantley's. They discovered that the twins were identical so that it was even difficult for Sarah and BB to tell them apart. Keily, Kevin, and James required all of Sarah's time and energy, though on weekends, especially Saturdays, BB took responsibility for all three while Sarah got ready for their special date. They hated to leave the children with a babysitter, but in order to maintain their sanity, once every two weeks, Idella, or someone from the church looked after them. Once William surprised Sarah with a trip to Toronto for a long weekend. Leaving the children for three days for the first time was torture for both of them, but they soon discovered they needed time to themselves every once in a while.

———◆◆◆◆———

William was comfortable with his position at Fuller & Sons. The twins were almost two when he became Executive Vice President of Design, a position that Earl Fuller created specifically for him. His basic design team was composed of the men on the assembly line who had grown to trust him over the years. They came up with ideas to make a better product, and it was William's job to find ways to implement them.

William was a key component of the executive team at Fuller. He had discovered years ago that Earl Fuller started every work day with his executive staff in the conference room with prayer. It was never a self-serving prayer, but just a simple prayer asking for a safe work day and that God would bless those who work at Fuller.

Yet, in his spare time, William yearned for something different; he wanted to start his own company, but had no idea what it would or should be. He knew two things—he wanted to stay in manufacturing, but it did not have to be in the same product line. He prayed often that God would provide him with such an opportunity.

"William, may I have a few minutes of your time?" He looked up and saw Earl Fuller framed by the open door to his office. Mr. Fuller was dressed in a white shirt with the sleeves rolled up. His hands were in his pockets.

"Certainly, Mr. Fuller, I mean Earl." Even though Earl Fuller insisted on being referred to as "Earl" by his executive team, William still slipped and called him "Mr. Fuller."

William followed Earl to his office. After the door was closed, the CEO opened a small refrigerator, grabbed two soft drinks and sat next to William on the couch before asking, "How long have you worked for us?" He handed one of the cans to William.

"Thank you," William nodded. "All together, around eight years," he answered.

"You know you can stay here as long as you want."

William nodded in agreement.

"Let's make this simple and then complex. Just before you graduated, I proposed that you work for us for a couple of years and then I would help you get started on your own. William, I intend to keep that promise whenever you are ready."

He paused and then went on to say, "I wouldn't be honest with you if I didn't tell you that I want you to stay. You have been a wonderful asset to Fuller, and my sons and I appreciate your hard work and dedication. We are impressed with your development of the vibration control process in the assembly machinery that reduces out-of-spec product by almost 80 percent. That has helped Fuller gain national recognition for quality control. And, as you well know, that sure boosts sales.

"However, to be true to myself and my belief structure, I must and will keep my promise open to you. That's what this little talk was going to be all about, that is until yesterday."

William knew it best to let his boss finish before responding.

"BB, yesterday morning I received confirmation that I have cancer, something our family physician suspected about a month ago."

Reacting to William's shocked expression, he continued, "Now before you go and get all riled up, let me finish. This is a second opinion and both sets of doctors claim it is terminal. According to them, I have no more than two years, tops."

William stammered, "Are you sure?"

"As sure as any doctors can get," he responded. "I've gone to the best—the first at UVA and finally the Mayo Clinic. Yes, with the advice I've received, I'm fairly certain.

"But, now to make this more complex. I know that

when I'm gone, the company will be in my sons' good hands. But, there are a couple of organizations that I have intended to associate Fuller with the last couple of years called Fellowship of Companies for Christ International, or FCCI, and C12. Well, I just never got around to it."

"With what you just told me, it's not difficult to understand," William replied.

Earl nodded acknowledgment before continuing, "You've heard the phrase, 'What Would Jesus Do?' Well, organizations like FCCI and C12 take that phrase into the workplace. To sum it up, I guess you can say that they offer means by which a company can truly become a platform for ministry and that has been my direction for Fuller for years; it's just that my efforts are so unstructured.

"Here is what I want to offer you. While I am going through this 'transition process,'" he formed quotation marks with his fingers, "I would like you to solidify my platform for ministry in the company, helping my sons with the transition. I want them to always remember that this company is rooted in Christ. I want them to understand that I do not want our wonderful people who work for us to feel they barter their lives just to stay alive money-wise or to preserve their family security. William, I don't want them going home everyday feeling that working for us dehumanizes them or their efforts. In other words, I want them to keep their souls and not sell them to us to make a dollar. And, with regard to my sons, the Bible has shown us so many times, the second generation tends to stray from allowing God to work in their lives. Having the resources of FCCI at their disposal and actively participating in a C12 group will keep them on track, that is, if I have done my job well.

"Now, William, I recognize that your background and experience is in business and engineering, but you have always shown a heart for the personal and spiritual needs of our people and, in particular, my sons. Ultimately that is more important than any product we sell."

Earl Fuller stood and walked to his desk. He picked up two folders and handed one to William. "This folder contains information about FCCI and C12. You will see some pretty impressive names on those rosters."

He handed William the second folder. "This, William, is what I will do for you if you stay and help my sons with this transition. It's fairly straightforward. Upon our reaching an agreement on this matter, you will receive enough stock in Fuller to leverage buying or starting your own company when you're finished here."

William sipped his Diet Coke and said nothing because he could not believe what he was reading and hearing.

"Now, take a look at the second set of papers in that folder. Not to be presumptuous, William, but Microtech Labs is the likes of something I think you should look into. Bill Talmadge, the GM over there, has been part of my Tuesday morning prayer group for a couple of years. Look, it's common knowledge around the plant that you have been dabbling in other applications for vibration controls. I do believe that is a major concern of the tech industry. Even though I am not that savvy about microprocessor fabrication, Bill has told me that in a process so delicate, vibration technology would be of great value."

He sat down next to his employee. "William, with some creative financing we can make it happen—you can either start your own company or buy one that would suit your needs. You decide. Take the materials back to your office, study them, talk to Sarah, and feel free to call Jack Coughlin, my financial advisor—just do what it takes. Then get back to me before Friday. I know this is out of the clear blue for you, but I have no doubt you can do what I'm asking here at Fuller and then start your own company. Just make sure that company is a platform for ministry as well. Agreed?"

In a daze, William walked back to his office, read through the materials, and finally picked up the telephone to call Sarah.

"Honey, you aren't going to believe what just happened and how God has answered our prayers."

<hr>

One evening a few months later, while he and Sarah were having dinner with Tony Hall and his wife, William confided how he felt that, even with all the support Mr. Fuller gave him, there was still something missing with regard to his commitment to the employees.

"Even though many of them have come to Christ, mostly through your guidance my friend," he tipped his glass in salute, "Fuller and Sons just can't keep up with caring for their employees and run the business at the same time. We are overextended to the point of exhaustion, and I'm afraid it's interrupting our own quality time with our families."

Tony acknowledged his salute with a nod of his head. "Have you ever considered hiring a corporate chaplain?"

"Not really," BB freely admitted.

"I can't question your commitment to your employees and your zeal to deliver Christ's message, but you can't do it yourself, not even with the help of the Fullers. The company has grown too much for that type of hands-on connection with everyone."

Tony took a sip of his coffee and continued, "There are several agencies that offer their services to companies that will do just what you said you and the Fullers are doing—caring for your employees in everyday family problems that they bring to the job. These chaplains are ordained ministers that help employees through such things as a death in the family, substance abuse, and financial difficulties—problems that carry over to the workplace. In some industries it could be cause for an unsafe environment. I'll put you in touch with some people that can help you out."

Two weeks later, with the blessing of Earl Fuller, BB contracted with a national agency to bring on Fuller and Sons' first corporate chaplain, Max Stauffer.

Six months later Mr. Fuller confided to BB that he was thrilled with the excellent care a corporate chaplain like Max brings to the workplace. Max became an integral part of the Fuller & Sons family.

In one of his last conversations with William, the

head of Fuller and Sons spoke in a raspy voice that resulted from his advanced cancer. "BB, I like the way Max visits our employees and family members in the hospital, conducts funerals, and provides crisis care that I, as the one who used to sign their paychecks, can no longer provide. I have already made arrangements with him to work with Pastor Miller to handle the service when I move on. "

BB answered, "Max has already asked me to put him in touch with your minister, Earl," BB choked back tears because this was one of the few times he had referred to Mr. Fuller by his first name without first being reminded to do so.

Noticing BB's touching response, Mr. Fuller reached out, hugged William, and whispered, "Finally pulled you in, did I? 'Mr. Fuller' is fine at the proper time, BB, but never when friends are alone. I'm glad Max has helped bring that out in you. We are all one big family, and I know that both of us have enjoyed our conversations with Max when he comes in on rounds. In particular I appreciate the concern Max has shown my family and me under the present circumstances."

Two years later, almost to the day he revealed to William that he had cancer, Earl Fuller died. BB sat in his boss's memorial service and reflected on his life since that day. The twins were almost five and Keily was in the first grade. When not with the brood, Sarah volunteered at a local church school for handicapped children. A passion had grown within her for giving her time to those less fortunate. Idella still played an important part in their lives. She had the common sense not to become so involved that she became a burden, but just involved enough so that when she came over the kids would be excited about seeing "Great Grammy."

William smiled as he thought, *Without her, I wouldn't be sitting here today. She had a wonderful knack for knowing how to push and prod when I needed it most, and yet she knew when to hold back so that I could discover on my own what was important to me, especially in planting the seeds of my faith.*

BB had worked closely with Mr. Fuller and his sons to establish an FCCI program at Fuller. He had also encouraged Mr. Fuller's eldest son, Rob, to join a C12 group. C12 groups had been established all around the United States by Buck Jacobs, an innovative business ministry entrepreneur. Each C12 group consisted of 12 business owners and a group facilitator called the group's "Chairman." They meet once a month for an entire day to help Christian business owners solve problems, share ideas, hold each other accountable, as well as work to build their companies as platforms for ministry to their employees and the community. Mr. Fuller knew that being part of the C12 group would help his sons greatly after he was no longer able to mentor them.

Working with Jack Coughlin, Fuller's financial advisor, William was able to develop an aggressive financial plan using the offered stock options and some of the saved insurance money to start his own laboratory. He discovered that Mr. Fuller was right; there was a tremendous need for reducing vibrations in the manufacturing of high-end computer chips. In his research, BB found out that a simple reduction of five to ten percent in out-of-spec product would save the industry hundreds of millions a year and give America a significant edge in the world market. This could save thousands of U.S. manufacturing jobs that might otherwise end up overseas.

Financially, developing the process would be tight, but Mr. Coughlin assured William that a two-year window was not unrealistic, that is if they focused on the process and did not become sidetracked. William was confident it could be done with the right people.

Sarah nudged William, bringing him back to the funeral service. He had been asked to say a few words on behalf of Mr. Fuller. While approaching the dais he reached into his pocket for the paper on which he had written the eulogy. He placed it on the pulpit and paused before he started reading, "Mr. Fuller was a giant in the manufacturing industry…" His words faded away as they seemed meaningless now. He paused, folded the sheets, and placed them back in his suit coat pocket.

He put his hands on each side of the pulpit for support and began, "What I was going to say about Earl Fuller was a list of his accomplishments on earth, but instead I want to talk about Earl Fuller, the man, God's servant. God wants us each to strive to live and serve Him as Jesus did. Earl Fuller is an example of how to do just that. Earl lived every day of his life, not for himself, but for the benefit of others and to serve God. Oh, he had his shortcomings just like all of us and don't we know them?" He looked at the Fuller men and their families who understood what William was alluding to. They laughed in unison as they each remembered various incidents, relieving some of their grief.

William continued, "However I would like to talk briefly about what Earl meant to me. As many of you are aware, my parents were killed in a car accident when I was five years old. My wonderful grandmother raised me, but I can honestly say that Earl was a close substitute to being a father, and I could not have had a better one."

With tears trickling down his cheeks, William talked for several more minutes about what Earl Fuller had meant to him. Idella sat next to Sarah. They both knew the significant impact Earl Fuller had on William and comforted each other at his loss by squeezing each other's hand.

They also realized the magnitude of William's saying goodbye to an old friend. This was the end of another chapter in William J. Brantley's life and the beginning of a new one.

Chapter 7

The Discovery

Money was tight in the Brantleys' world once again. It had been two years since Mr. Fuller had died, and William's little company, Brantley and Associates, consisting of six people, was struggling for money. Every one of them believed that they were so close to creating a vibration reduction process for high end computer chips that they worked for reduced salaries, banking on the future, sure they were within striking distance of their goal.

They designed silicone gel-cushioned joints, worktables, armatures, and complete assembly lines, which they field tested but could never quite achieve the high standard of vibration reduction they had set for themselves. Flush with cash and desperate for manufacturing efficiencies due to capacity constraints, chip producers showed a strong interest in the product line. In their minds, any vibration reduction could mean more money on the bottom line. B & A, however, was reluctant to go beyond product prototypes because, even though their invention showed strong promise, BB knew the final breakthrough lay still ahead.

However, within six months, a Chinese firm was duplicating the process and manufacturing the joints, worktables, armatures, and assembly lines in large quantities to support an exponentially growing market. William and his associates had realized that this could happen, but not as quickly as it did. The Chinese were known for their capacity to duplicate American technology, whether in textiles, furniture, or computer chips. When they saw an opportunity to grab a world market, they did it, and the result was thousands of lost jobs, often in the United States. They produced B & A's product far less expensively than William and his team ever could.

William knew they were on the verge of a great breakthrough, but an ingredient was missing and he could not figure out what it was. One evening, he finally told Sarah about the business's plight before going to bed. Her answer was simple: "Pray." They prayed together, holding hands, before retiring.

The next evening after dinner when William was playing with Keily, Kevin, and James in the family room, the doorbell rang. It was almost Christmas time and UPS was working overtime to meet the delivery rush. A large box arrived for Sarah from her parents labeled, "Open Immediately." Inside, to her delight, was a large canister of gourmet popcorn, but more to the glee of the children was the bubble wrap that encased it. Sarah and William shared the kids' joy as they jumped on the wrap and burst the pockets of air with a loud "pop!" They all laughed until they almost cried.

William had trouble sleeping that night because he was trying to find answers to the problems B & A was facing. Frustrated, he tried to distract himself by thinking about the fun they all had earlier with the bubble wrap. He chuckled as he remembered that when they landed on the cushion of air, it was followed by the expected explosion with the release of plastic encased gas. *Why can't our process be that simple?* he thought. Suddenly the answer he had been seeking so long and hard came to him. *And, why not?* He grabbed the telephone and called Tom Dussell, his chief design engineer. "Call the guys and meet me at the lab!"

When Tom Dussell, Gwen Theibert, Andrew White, and Tim Kearney arrived at the plant, they found William setting up a demonstration in the production lab. On the counter next to the sink, the coffee pot was steaming. BB had a Diet Coke in one hand and an insulin syringe in the other. He had placed several of the silicone cushioned joints in line on the table. After they each grabbed a hot cup of coffee, William began to explain the revelation he received after watching the kids play with the bubble wrap.

While they watched with anticipation, BB injected one of the silicone joints with the air in the hypodermic needle. The resultant stream of bubbles was evident in the silicone. He placed a dab of high tech adhesive they used to hold the joints together on the pinprick hole and blew on it to dry.

After two minutes, he turned to Dussell and said,

"Tom, check this out for vibration level reduction, please."

Dussell gingerly inserted the module in the grips of the vibration table. He turned on the motors and watched the monitor paint a smooth, even picture across the screen. He quickly recalibrated, increasing the sensitivity. Dussell let out a long, wavering shout. "You guys are not going to believe this. Look! Almost a 15 percent vibration reduction! That's what we've been looking for! There is no way the Chinese can match that."

B & A erupted into loud shouts of approval. His associates gave each other "high fives," and kept crying out, "You've done it! BB, you've done it!"

William looked at each rejoicing face and said, "No, my friends, *we've* done it with God's help."

Once the celebration died down, they agreed to spend the rest of the night refining the process to see if they could further reduce the vibrations. By sunrise they had exceeded their goal of 15 percent vibration reduction by varying the amount of air injected into the modules.

Gwen finally asked the question, "What about the work tables, armatures, and assembly lines? Do we use the same process with them?"

Andrew responded, "I think we should do the work and test them, but let's put one item on the market at a time. We already beat the others' reduced vibration levels with just the cushioned joints."

Tim chimed in, "I agree and I think I've got a way to keep our work from being copied beyond the protection of a patent." He spent the better part of three hours showing his partners how to protect their God-sent product.

William said, "Let's stop right now and thank God for this incredible idea." BB then bowed his head as the others followed his example. "Father God, thank You for blessing us with everything we needed to develop this process. May your blessings help us to build Your kingdom. In Jesus' name we pray. Amen."

———◆∙◈∙◆———

Over the next five years, B & A Manufacturing became immensely successful with their vibration reduction technology in full production, gaining them recognition throughout the world. They grew from the original six to 657 employees. Their product line expanded, supporting vibration reduction in hundreds of different close tolerance manufacturing applications. As a result, BB became a rising star, not only on the national scene, but also internationally. Those who worked with him acknowledged and appreciated his work ethic, as well as his concern for the well-being of his employees.

William never forgot the tenets taught him by Earl Fuller. He introduced FCCI to his growing employee base within the first year the production company was established. He met with his executive team on a daily basis. Early in their struggling years when they were trying to develop the vibration reduction technology, William had introduced them to Sarah and his evangelist friend, Tony Hall. Every five or six weeks at BB's request, Tony would lead a prayer group of six key people as they sought God's direction. Within a year they had all come to accept Jesus Christ as their personal Lord and Savior.

William, Tony, and the others formed a bond in Christ that made them inseparable. They were all active in their respective community churches, but they each relied on Tony for in-depth spiritual guidance.

As the company grew, BB found that it could be very lonely at the top as the firm's corporate leader, even though he spent a significant amount of his time learning about his employees, especially those who worked on the manufacturing floor. Walking in the steps of Earl Fuller, he made every effort to learn about their families, if they were willing to share with him. He never forced the issue and was careful not to pry into their private affairs. His goal was for them to feel comfortable when he was present, and eventually BB became quite adept at small talk.

He was thankful for his contacts through FCCI and the other members of his C12 group, and that his executive team approved of his active participation. He enjoyed going to meetings and conferences with his associates where they developed relationships with other executives and company leaders. Through these relationships, his team was encouraged by witnessing God working, not only in their own company, but in other corporations as well.

Over the next two years, with the support of his leadership team and guidance from Tony, William brought not only most of B & A's employees, but also a significant number of their peers in the business world, to Christ. William's reputation as a Christian business leader was growing. News media began to do stories on this "corporate leader who personally displays a magnificent sense of balance, connecting his spirituality and his corporate judiciousness," as reported by Fox News correspondent, Shirley Williamson.

———◆•◆•◆———

One evening, after sharing Sarah's delicious, home-cooked meal with frequent house guest Tony Hall, William began to reflect back on some of the things that made his company operate head and shoulders above the competition.

William turned to Tony and asked, "Do you remember our conversation when I was at Fuller and I felt that something was still missing with regard to our commitment to our Fuller employees? Lots of them had come to Christ, mostly through your efforts, my friend, but we couldn't keep up with all their needs. We were all tired and I was afraid if we continued at the pace we were going, we would end up as needy as some of our employees."

"BB, I think I told you that you needed a corporate chaplain, something you had no inkling even existed."

"Yes, and I said I was not so sure Fuller could afford one. Yet, once you explained the concept to Mr. Fuller, he jumped on board immediately and turned out to be the biggest supporter. In fact, he admitted he used Max as his own personal chaplain when he was diagnosed with cancer, he trusted him so much. That was some of the best advice you gave me in those days. As a result, even with money as tight as it was, the leadership team and I recognized having a chaplain was an essential component in the care and growth of our associates."

"I have never questioned your commitment to your employees at both Fuller and at B & A," Tony replied. "I think the wisest lesson you learned at Fuller was that you can't do it all yourself." Tony laughed. "I remember saying, 'Ye of little faith. God will provide for the funding of the chaplain, all you have to do is trust in Him.'" Tony smiled as he continued. "Followed by something like, 'Put your money where your mouth is, BB, and give them a try.'"

"I remember the first week we contracted to bring Tom Shaffer on as our corporate chaplain at B & A after our business mushroomed overnight. Tom began to make the rounds and build relationships with both the employees and company leaders. I'd say that Tom earned his keep the first six months he was with us."

"Oh yeah, I remember when the acid bath boiled over and splattered on that young woman."

"It was Kelly Oswald. Even though she had the presence of mind to douse herself at the emergency shower, the splash also affected her face because she didn't have on her protective shield. Tom met the emergency vehicle at the hospital. When they discovered that she might be scarred for life, he was right there for her and her entire family for almost six weeks, helping them adjust. Then, to boot, Tom spent another major part of his time caring for those who assisted Kelly in the emergency. They were as shook up as her family. I would never have had the time nor the words that would minister like he did."

"Yeah, BB, corporate chaplains are men and women who not only have a gift to minister to people in crises, but they have received training to fine tune their gift," Tony said. "Because Tom was trained for the task, he's always able to provide genuine caring in the workplace. He often says there are four Cs associated with great corporate chaplaincy: confidentiality, competency, compassion, and most of all, the love of Christ.

"Gladys Bennett is another example of his effective ministry."

"Don't you know it," BB agreed. "Designing those chaplain calling cards the employees carry in their wallets with the emergency number was pure genius. When her husband had a heart attack while they were on vacation, Gladys called Tom on the 800 number. Tom took over from this end and saw that a pastor was contacted close to Gladys who helped from that end. Then when Herman passed on, Tom helped her make arrangements to fly his remains back home from Alaska. When she arrived back here, Tom met Gladys at the airport and helped her and her family work through their grief. Tom's handling of the funeral arrangements, as well as performing the service—well, we couldn't ask for anymore, could we?"

"As large as your company has become, BB, the chaplaincy program ensures your employees are still cared for as individuals. And they are so thankful you think enough about them that you would care for their needs, whatever they may be. You have made Christ first in this business, and it especially shows through the ministry of the corporate chaplain."

"I don't think God would have it any other way," BB took another sip of his Diet Coke, "No sir, He would not have it any other way."

Chapter 8

Countdown

William and Sarah were now in their 40s, and one particular evening they were enjoying a quiet time together at home. He peaked over the pages of the journal he was reading and watched his wonderful wife of more than 20 years reading next to him on the sofa. Sarah's legs were curled underneath her, and her left elbow was propped on the armrest. She was deeply engrossed in the latest Christian fiction novel. *I could watch her like this for hours,* he thought. *God has given me the perfect mate and three wonderful children. The twins are seventeen and Keily...* his thoughts jolted him into action.

"Sarah, the twins are going to be following Keily to college this time next year. We've got to start planning where they're going to go."

Sarah smiled and looked over at him. "I believe we had this conversation last week, Honey. The boys have started working with the counselors at school trying to narrow down their choices. Kevin wants to go to a small college. I think he wants to own his own business like you. James has taken a keen interest in science the last two years. He keeps hinting about a career of some sort in the medical field."

BB let out a sigh of relief. "I'm sorry, Sarah. Sometimes, I feel like a klutz around here. I know what the kids and you are doing almost all of the time, but somehow I feel like I'm missing something."

"You could say that for me, too," she responded. She paused, moved down the sofa and snuggled next to him. "I think it's because they've grown up so fast that it seems like it's happened in the blink of an eye. One day, we're putting a bandage on Keily's skinned knee and the next we're buying her a prom dress. Sometimes it just doesn't seem fair. But, that's the way God has designed it to be, and we have to learn to let them go."

She removed his reading glasses and kissed him on the forehead. "But some things don't change." She put the spectacles on the coffee table and wrapped her arms around him thinking, *It can't get any better than this.*

As she looked into his eyes, she added, "BB, you have had a lot on your plate the last few years, in particular with that Chinese corporation trying to figure out how to duplicate your reduction process. Hearing about industrial espionage to me is like reading a good thriller, but you have to deal with it in the real world, an entirely different matter."

"I know, Honey, but Tom solved that problem from the beginning. Maybe it's just the pressure of knowing sooner or later they will discover the key to the process, I don't know. But why would Kim Khiang Wee,

International Asian Machinery's CEO, invite me to go there to speak before some large Chinese manufacturing consortium? Kim wants me to talk about how B & A got started, our management style, and insights on why we have been so successful. With all the political tension between the U.S. and China, I'm not sure our government will let me go anyway. According to LC, the Department of Labor and the State Department are very concerned about this trip. He thinks Kim just wants to get me over there to see if they can trick me or even force me into revealing the secrets to our process."

He paused. "Who would ever have thought my college buddy, LC Cunningham, would have been so successful in government work, especially in the CIA?"

"You've been friends all these years. You can trust his judgment, BB, but is there a way to work around this bump in the road?"

"Some government officials are concerned that my speech will be used for propaganda purposes to try to portray U.S.-Chinese relations as being much better than they really are. Others, like LC, think that all the Chinese care about is getting me over there in order to steal our process technologies. Apparently, this whole thing has become a huge geopolitical battle. Heck, I'm just a business guy wanting to do the right thing.

"LC said yesterday that both sides are close to signing an agreement that would allow me to speak at the conference, so long as my entire talk is aired live and unedited on Chinese national television. Our guys say this will keep the Chinese from using me as a propaganda tool because it's difficult to spin a live speech, and the Chinese say it will prove that they have no such intentions." BB paused, his brows knit together. "If it all works out, we will have to assume that God is in it, and we should commit to go. At least that's the way I'm praying about it."

"As Grammy always says," Sarah ran her fingers through his hair, "God put you on this planet for a reason and maybe His hand is in this."

The next morning William J. Brantley would realize the wisdom of his wife's words.

———•✦•———

"BB," Tony Hall's voice echoed over the speaker phone, "Did you know that there are 1,271,884,000 Muslims in the world today, that's almost 1.3 billion and growing? Now stack that up against 242,697,000 evangelical Christians—we've got to do something about it."

"I thought that's what we've been working on."

"On a small scale, my friend, on a small scale. We've got to think big."

BB asked, "Tony, what brought this on? I mean this is out of nowhere."

"Your trip to China. Ever since you told me about the invitation, I've been mulling it over, mostly out of concern for you, especially your safety. I can't remember when I've prayed over something as much as I have this little overseas jaunt you're proposing to take."

"Yeah, that is if the feds will let me go. I've got to work around some of the issues before I can go with their blessing," BB replied.

"Oh, you're going, my friend. I see God at work in this, and if it's what He wants—well, you're going and you will be safe," Tony replied.

"Now where was I?" Tony asked. "Ah yes," he continued. "It's just that I could not see 'the forest for the trees.' I was asking God all the wrong questions. The direction came to me last night as I prayed for His complete protection if you go. The answer was staring me in the face on my desk, even as I prayed."

"I know I sound excited, BB, but the last few weeks I have been tracking comparative numbers of those involved with various worldwide religions. The study was lying on my desk while I was praying for you. We've got to catch up, my friend; we've really got to catch up."

For the next hour, Tony explained China was potentially the answer to a worldwide Christian revival or awakening. "There was no major spiritual awakening during the 20th century. Oh, there were a couple of spikes here and there, but nothing in comparison to the numbers generated during the 1700s or 1800s. Even with the Billy Graham and Billy Sunday crusades, the Jesus Movement, groups like Promise Keepers, and all the people who came to Christ during the two world wars, there was still no major spiritual awakening during the 20th century."

"So, what does China have to do with a worldwide revival?" BB asked. "Christians there are persecuted more than any other place in the world."

"That's my point. Surprisingly, more than 10,000 Chinese are coming to Christ on a weekly basis under those horrific conditions. They live in fear and have to sneak around and meet in houses, just like the early Christians. That's 520,000 new Christians in just one year's time. Good numbers, but God may be opening an even greater door of opportunity here. How many people will you be speaking to on their national television network?"

"Not quite a million, Tony," BB reminded him. "Why?"

"I think it's possible to reach one billion people with the gospel message," he paused, "in a—in a 72-hour period of time."

"You're crazy!"

———◆•◆•◆———

During the next several months, William prayed with Sarah, Grammy, B & A's corporate chaplain Tom, Tony, and a few other trusted friends as to what direction to take. LC Cunningham was running interference for him in Washington.

"Look, BB," LC said, "this has really gotten dicey. The war on terror has my bosses concerned about you and your safety. Look at the number of American journalists and business people who have been kidnapped and assassinated in every part of the world. Not that I am trying to talk you out of going; it's not that at all. BB, putting aside all this political mumbo jumbo, I'm concerned for your safety. I just don't want to lose another friend. I hope you can see that."

"I understand, LC, but it's something I feel God

wants me to do. With you covering my back, what else could I ask for?"

"Now, to your language concerns," LC continued. "I think I have that resolved, and I believe my solution will knock their socks off, that is if you are up to a challenge?"

BB thought back on his uneasiness about sharing his faith in Christ on Chinese television. If he did, he thought the Chinese might shut him down immediately and the message would not be delivered. Also, Tony told him about his experience with several crusades overseas. Tony had discovered that, even when he was in his best evangelistic mode, many times he was not very effective speaking through translators who were unable to communicate not only his enthusiasm about Jesus Christ but also the depth of his message. "I guess you could say that my charisma gets lost in the translation," he joked with BB on several occasions. "You have to be aware of that possibility, my friend."

LC drew BB back to the present by saying, "We will be sending a security detail with you."

"Is that necessary?"

"It most certainly is. Look, the guys that will be assigned will just look like a bunch of suits tagging along with you to see Beijing. They won't be as obvious as the Secret Service surrounding the President because no one will be on the lookout for them. But, BB, let's just say I'm going to work hard to cover all our bases. The treaty has been signed, and the speech will be aired live on Chinese national TV. If anyone pulls the plug, there will be heck to pay on both sides."

LC went on to share his heart with his friend. When he told BB how he had come to Christ after 9/11, William gave a whoop. "Why didn't you tell me this sooner, LC? I can't wait to share this with Sarah. We have prayed for years for you."

"I wish I had, but I guess I felt intimidated by my level of biblical knowledge as compared to you or Tony. I guess I just saw myself as another guy working a government job. Now I see that God has always had a plan for my life and I'm watching it unfold daily. It's amazing to see God work out all the details for your speech. From here on out, though, I'm in the game for real. I have every intention of going to China with you."

———◆•◆•◆———

While negotiations continued between the two state departments, William studied past revivals or spiritual awakenings and the impact they had on shaping history. He found out that the first great awakening served its purpose in the colonies when they were headed toward becoming a nation. Breaking away from England would not come easy and required great effort by the colonists. During the Civil War the Christian Commission, as well as many other such organizations, kept the spiritual revival alive during very trying times when brother fought against brother.

"The more I read, the more in awe I am of what you're suggesting, Tony," BB shared at lunch one day. "You're talking about something seemingly out of the realm of possibility, especially over a 72-hour period.

These revivals took years, not days," BB reminded his mentor.

"So what? If God was able to create the world in six days and rest on the seventh, who can say He can't do what we're considering? Remember, BB, we're only His conduit to work in this world He has so graciously given us. If we listen to Him, He'll work through us and we can give Him all the credit. Though history books might say it was you, Christians will know the truth. It *can* be done. You just have to accept your assignment and move forward."

William leaned back in his chair, hands behind his head. "You know I'm going to do this, Tony, and I'm not afraid. My only concerns are for Sarah and the kids if something was to go wrong, God forbid."

"You said it. Who else better to cover your back than God Himself? He certainly has put LC in the right place at the right time. That guy is doing great now that he's come out of hiding.

"Let's move onto some more practical matters. Did you talk with your IT director about coming up with a tracking process so we know if we've been successful?"

BB handed Tony a memo from Tom Dussell who had his team working on Tony's request.

Memo to: BB
From: TD
Subject: Operation Beijing Tracking

I think our Web Development team has arrived at

a solution that will accommodate the large numbers of anticipated hits on the site and can be independently audited. To handle the anticipated traffic, they've created multiple paths to the registration page using redundant servers and mirrored ISP sites. Additionally, Fowler, Freburg, and Howell has agreed to provide independent auditing to substantiate the results for the event.

"Sounds like a lot of slick computereze to me. Will it work?"

"If Tom Dussell says it will work, it will work. After all, he's been able to keep our vibration reduction process from the Chinese all these years, and that's why we've been invited to China in the first place. I'm sure they somehow think they can entice me to give them the process. If I know Tom, he has everything all set up and ready to go as we speak."

The night before leaving for China, BB lay in bed staring at the familiar patterns created on the ceiling by the ambient light from the streetlight. Listening to her irregular breathing patterns, he could tell Sarah was not sleeping either. He was thinking about the high stakes that were riding on this trip they were about to take. Few people had been told the real purpose of BB's accepting the invitation. *But I want to succeed,* he thought. *I want to succeed.* He let out a long sigh.

"Can't sleep either," Sarah softly whispered into his

ear. He had not noticed that she had turned toward him, watching his every move.

"I'm sorry if I'm keeping you awake. I guess the excitement is getting to me."

"I'd be excited too if I were you," she spoke as she placed her arm across his chest and snuggled closer.

"Why can't you sleep?" BB asked, concerned that she would be exhausted the next day.

Sarah sat up and hugged the covers to her chest before saying, "Honestly, BB, I have supported you on everything you've ever done—even to putting Grammy into Sunnyside against her wishes. I know how hard that was for you, but I knew it had to be done for her sake."

"Yeah, but look at her today, a little over two years there and she actually likes it there. The last time I talked with her she went on and on about this new friend and that new friend."

"I know it broke your heart and when your heart breaks, mine feels the same pain." She paused. "But even though on the outside I have supported this trip, deep down inside of me I'm scared, not only for you, but selfishly for the kids and...and...me. First, you know my feelings about flying, and we're going to be in the air a long time. Add to that these worldwide terrorist activities and I'm petrified. Keily will be here with the twins, but if something should happen to us..." her voice trailed off.

"You're not being selfish, Sarah." BB gently pulled her close to him. "I'm concerned too, not only about the flight, but what if we fail. I keep trying to convince myself that only a few people will know, but God will and He's the One I am trying to please, not me, not Tony, not you. LC's worried about what might happen while we're there. There are too many kidnappings and assassinations going on worldwide for his comfort level."

"But if you don't try, we'll never know, will we?" she asked. "I just want you to understand I'm kind of the reverse picture of a hyena. I heard it said that they look sad on the outside, but are always laughing on the inside. Well, I'm laughing on the outside and crying on the inside, but only God and you know."

"Do you want to stay home?" he asked.

"Yes and no. Even though I'm shaking in my shoes, I'm going. I'm not going to miss a chance to watch my most favorite person in the world share Jesus with those lost souls in China. As far as I'm concerned, if you bring just one person to Jesus while we're there, you'll have been successful. It's in God's hands now, and He never fails."

"Truer words were never spoken, and that's why I love you." He uncurled his arm around her and took her hands in his. "Let's thank Him for bringing us this far and ask his continued blessings on what we're about to do." He squeezed her hands tightly as they prayed. "What better security can we ask for?" BB said as they slid under the covers once more to try to sleep.

Thirty-six hours later Sarah and BB were admiring the sights of Beijing on their way to the hotel. Even though they used every process known to man to avoid jet lag, including using a government issued jet arranged by LC, they still suffered. LC and his six man security detail arrived fresh, however.

LC explained, "Hey, that's our job to stay alert and to keep you guys from getting into trouble. We're used to making the adjustment. Just get yourselves acclimated."

Even though LC had made the connections in order to guarantee the safety of Sarah and BB, B & A's CEO insisted on paying the tab for their transportation and lodging out of his own pocket to avoid any impropriety. "It will rest a lot easier with me," BB insisted. "I was and still am a little concerned about the precedent this will set, but I will be more comfortable if you can show the government I paid every penny for this trip, which in turn takes you off the hook, LC."

———••••••———

The Chinese were gracious hosts. They did not overlook any detail to make their visitors comfortable. Mr. Kim Khiang Wee, CEO of International Asian Machinery, met them at the airport and provided limousine service to the Beijing Hilton.

"Look at this—this room—suite—palace!" Sarah exclaimed, still a little groggy from the affects of the mild tranquilizer her doctor had prescribed for the flight. She ran over and jumped on the super king-sized bed, unaware that LC and his crew were stealthily screening for surveillance devices in all their suites. During the flight he explained that, unfortunately, once on the ground all conversations would have to be guarded because of the possibility of bugs everywhere.

"Limos, hotel rooms, restaurants, even at the conference they will have long and short range devices to overhear our conversations. So once we are on the ground, we'll talk only about family, friends, and business associates. Even though my guys and I will probably not understand any of the shop talk, we'll make it up as we go so they will view us as just part of your corporate team."

LC was not surprised that their suite was full of bugs. He had told BB in Washington two weeks before the trip, "They are interested in a little industrial espionage and want to get as many details as they can about your process. Just throw up some 'red herrings' to satisfy them and leave it at that. If you give them something they think is important, it will lessen the chance they'll try to get more directly from you."

In the days prior to the trip, BB's development team gave him all the information he needed to send the Chinese industrialists off on a wild goose chase for at least another two to three years. At every opportunity that presented itself while they were in China, BB and his team gave a well-rehearsed "Tom Dussell pitch," being careful not to overdo it.

———◆◆◆◆◆———

"I can't believe how courteous everyone is here!" a delighted Sarah exclaimed. "They can't do enough for you. They struggle with their English, but who am I to criticize. I'm the foreigner here, yet they try to speak my language. I wish I could speak a second language, don't you, BB?"

"Oh, LC has taught me a little Mandarin, the standard language throughout China," BB said as he winked at the CIA agent. He continued, "It's just like the United States, we have our various accents, southern, western, and New England; their different localities here have assorted dialects. But they all understand Mandarin. So we don't have to worry about the translation of my talk tomorrow night, that is unless they don't like what I have to say about how we operate our business and discovered the process for vibration reduction." BB freely said he was going to divulge all the Chinese wanted in his speech.

They were riding in the second car of several limos that were escorting them around the Chinese capital.

"You talk about how nice this city is, Sarah," LC said, "but it's also a technology savvy city. There are well over 3 million Internet subscribers in Beijing alone, which is about 12.5 percent of the country's total. That's a lot of computers. I suppose computer access is limited in the outlying areas, but in the cities, millions have access."

"Not to change the subject, but how close are we to the Convention Center? I would like to see what it looks like from the outside. Could we just drive by?" BB asked.

Hu Banghong, their driver and guide who was fluent in English, told them he would be glad to show them. As he drove he took on the role of a tour guide. "The Beijing International Convention Center specializes in staging national and international conferences, exhibitions, and other large state events. It has 77,000 square meters of usable space."

The guide continued his speech while the group listened intently. Sarah watched as they drove by the National Olympic Sports Center located across the street from the BICC. She was thrilled when they drove through Tiananmen Square where history was made when a Chinese boy stood in front of a huge tank for the whole world to see as he defied the Chinese government.

The next morning BB went through a sound check on stage. He was surrounded by technicians who wore microphones and several translators who wanted to hear him speak so they could become familiar with the cadence of his presentation. He was assured that it would help the translators convey the dynamism of his speech to the audience, and those watching on television and hearing it broadcast on radio or even the Internet. BB hoped so.

The dress rehearsal went off without any glitches; BB was ready to talk. He had only one more arrangement to make and that was to send a bouquet of flowers to Grammy for her 91st birthday. He wanted to be there, but she understood the importance of what he was doing in the name of Christ. Using his laptop computer he ordered the largest arrangement he could find for her and signed the card, "Wish I could be there. I know you understand. All my love. BB." He loved teasing her by using the nickname that was off limits when he was in her presence. "Just to keep your blood flowing," he would kid her.

Chapter 9

The Speech

As Sarah, BB, LC, and his group walked to the preparation room where they could relax for a few moments before the presentation, they noticed the Convention Center was filled to capacity. Their gracious host, Kim Khiang Wee, had told them that interest level in William's speech had exceeded all expectations. Not only were there manufacturing industrialists represented, but the controversy surrounding a successful U.S. businessman speaking unedited in China caught the curiosity of the general public. In an effort to capitalize on the appearance of eased tensions between the super powers, the Chinese government had made a considerable effort to publicize the event. As a result, corporate China was excited to hear William speak about his business success in America.

BB paced the floor as he thought that, for the most part, their visit in China had been pleasant, except for the times he was in meetings with the Chinese manufacturing corporate sector and they tried to wrangle BB's process for vibration reduction out of him.

At one point, after a long PowerPoint presentation on the success and strength of Chinese industry, they offered to produce the various parts from the cushioned joints to the work tables and ship them at a good price to B & A for sales. "This is what you in America call a 'win-win' situation, and we all make money," Wee said with a smile.

"What do I do with our loyal employees whose very livelihoods depend on their making these same products for us for sale?" BB asked. "No, I think our company is satisfied with what we are doing financially. I am very sorry, but I must respectfully decline your generous offer," BB said without any hesitation.

"There is no doubt that you can produce a quality product for less," he continued, "but our corporate bottom line is not just to make as much money as we can for our company." BB explained to a baffled audience, "Of course, we would not be able to exist if we did not profit from the product, but we also are in the market to produce jobs for our employees that will give them a a good quality of life, which, in turn, will help us grow our company.

"My wife and I, along with my associates, cannot thank you enough for your hospitality during our time in your beautiful city. After my presentation tonight, we will be headed back to the United States with nothing but pleasant memories. Again, we are in your debt and would like to invite you to come to the United States for a similar opportunity."

LC, who was sitting next to BB, cringed at the offer, but no one noticed. *I know he's being gracious,* LC thought, *but he should have cleared that through the State Department and the Department of Labor. Nothing will come of it, I'm sure, but he's skating on thin ice here.*

———◆◆◆———

Sarah took William's hand in hers, which brought the evening's keynote speaker back to the present. "Nervous?" she asked.

"Like a cat in a room full of rocking chairs," he grinned. "This is so important, and I must not fail."

"You'll do fine. God has gotten you this far, and He will carry you the rest of the way," she calmly said. "Be careful not to pinch your skin," she said in reference to BB's propensity to massage the fold between his thumb and forefinger when giving a speech.

"That should be the least of your worries," he said. "I've got so much nervous sweat running down my legs into my shoes that I'm afraid they'll hear me sloshing as I walk to the podium." He laughed, and much to the surprise of the Chinese representatives, he pulled up his pant leg to cool himself off.

"All right, smarty, I don't know what protocol you just breached, but I get the message," she playfully slapped the back of his offending hand.

As he smoothed out his pants leg, he asked his Chinese hosts if he and his group could have a private moment. After they were alone, he asked the team to form a circle and hold hands. "Let's have a moment of prayer," he said as they bowed their heads. "Heavenly

Father, thank You for this trip and for the opportunity to share our business plan here in China. Please be with each of us as we continue on this journey that You have planned and brought about. We pray in Jesus' name. Amen."

A slight knock on the door indicated it was time for his presentation. Sarah and the others left BB alone with his thoughts as they went out and took their box seats.

The convention stage was awash with bright lights as BB and Mr. Wee approached center stage. BB took his assigned seat as Wee took the podium. For almost ten minutes, Wee read William's resume before he presented him to the audience. As William approached the dais, he looked up at Sarah and in a manner only she would see, turned his wedding ring on his finger to show his love for her and that he was ready to do what he had gone there to do.

"Thank you, Mr. Wee, for your kind hospitality the last few days," he paused for the translation. "My wife, friends, and associates thank you also." For the next few moments he went through the pleasantries associated with the beginning of a formal presentation. Even though he had practiced with the translators, William found that waiting on the audience's reaction to the translators was a little unnerving.

On the other side of the world, thousands of miles away, Idella Brantley was excited. She kept looking at the clock on her microwave. It said 8:37 am, one minute later than the last time she had looked. She busied herself with cleaning places that did not need to be cleaned; her apartment was spotless. She refolded clothes that did not need to be folded and rearranged drawers that were already neat as a pin. Once again, she looked at the time. "It's only 8:38," she mumbled. *Excitement sure causes time to slow down,* she thought.

Idella had every right to be excited. Today, actually in China, tonight, at 9:00 pm, William was going to appear on Chinese national television. Only he and a few of his closest business partners knew what he was going to say, but he had confided in Grammy a month before when he visited with her.

"I can't help but believe God wants to take my words and, with His power, use them to lead millions to eternal life, Grammy," he had said. "I know that this is part of God's purpose for me."

He grasped her hand as he continued, "If you had not made sure that I was in the right place at the right time, especially being deeply involved in the church, I would not be here today. You, as well as others," he paused and smiled, "but most importantly, you laid a firm foundation for my faith. Without that foundation I might never have come to Christ or done any of the things He's allowed me to do. I guess we could say that was your purpose."

Grammy caressed his hand as she loved to do. "You came to Christ on your own. The night Sarah and you called and told me that you had given your lives to Him," she choked back tears, "was an overwhelming answer to prayer for me. In a way I guess you could say that I was selfish because that night I knew that all of us—your grandfather, mother, father, me, and yes, Sarah—would be together for eternity, but in God's plan, not ours."

"Personally, I don't dwell that much on heaven and what it's going to be like," he said. "Yes, I know we'll all be together, but the glory that God has in store for us is way beyond my comprehension. Our feeble minds cannot fathom His eternal plan for each of us, so why waste energy trying to figure it out? I was put here on earth to serve God as best as I can. When I came to Christ that evening I knew that my past sins had been forgiven, and heaven would be the end of my journey. As I've matured, I've discovered that there will always be meaning to our lives. God saved us to serve Him, and that's what counts."

Bringing herself back to the present, Idella looked again at the time and saw it was 8:59. "Finally." She lowered her head and prayed for her dear William.

"Idella," a gentle voice interrupted her. "You've done your job well...I'll help him from here. It's time for you to rest now." She looked up and saw a figure in dazzling white standing next to her. Startled, she asked, "Who are you?"

He smiled, "That's always the first question I get asked. I guess it's better than *what* are you?" He patted her hand. "To William, I was Big Mike. To you I was his phantom friend. Later, I was Miguel Estrada and Professor Mickey Dugan, and Brother Mick at the hospital. You see, William has an important role to play in

God's plan, and my mission has been to take special care of him."

"You're Michael the archangel!" Grammy exclaimed. "You've been with him all these years, haven't you?"

"Only when he needed me, and tonight I'll stand with him again...after I take care of a very special errand. Are you ready to go, Idella?"

"I'm ready to meet Him if that's what you're asking."

The mighty archangel took hold of her right hand as her left slipped off the armrest. She allowed herself a last glance at William's family portrait on the wall. "Goodbye," she said and because she was so proud of William she called him a name she had never called him before, "I love you, BB." Idella was on her way to meet Jesus, and in the blinking of an eye, Michael the archangel was at William's side.

William was speaking to a major portion of China's over 1.5 billion citizens. He was appearing in the Beijing International Convention Center, one of the largest such venues in the world. He was dwarfed by the size of the stage, even with all the politicos that surrounded him.

After his introductory remarks, he began his speech on vibration reduction technology and what its introduction to the computer world had meant. He talked about B & A's corporate philosophy and how the most important part of the company were the individuals who produced their product.

Those listening all over China could only hear what

William was saying through the drone of translators. They could not hear the passion in his voice. His lips moved, but they only heard a translation.

William moved confidently through the first part of his speech, which lasted only ten minutes. However, he faltered as he began to make the transition: "There is a second part to my talk this evening..."

"Oh no. BB's hand is not in his pocket. He's got to get his hand in his pocket to get through this," LC said through clenched teeth. "Come on, BB, do what we practiced so hard." LC said a silent prayer for BB's clarity of mind.

"Why are you worried that his hand's not in his pocket?" Sarah asked LC. "What does that have to do with giving a speech?"

As she asked the question, Sarah saw the wind blow that always recalcitrant wisp of hair on BB's forehead into place. Almost immediately his hand slipped into his pocket. Sarah was astonished at what happened next.

On the huge stage, William was struggling, not because of the message he was giving, but the enormity of the task God had set out for Him to do. However, as his right hand slid into his pocket, he began to speak in almost perfect Mandarin, which translated into English was, "...and this is what Jesus Christ means to me, my friends, family, and business."

As William continued his well-rehearsed speech, the translators looked confused as did the politicians and corporate leaders sharing the stage with him.

In other state-controlled venues such as radio and television stations, supervisors were screaming to cut the feed. Each time the technicians tried to follow orders, dials and control panels that had been in perfect working order could not be turned off or muted. Communications between supervisors and operators deteriorated quickly into anger and confusion as they struggled to stop the broadcast; others in the studios seemed so dumfounded that they could only move in slow motion and were unable to respond to direction.

William pressed on calmly, reaching into his inside jacket pocket for his well-worn Bible. With Michael invisibly by his side, BB never hesitated or faltered during the entire presentation and seemed at ease finding and reading the passages he had chosen.

"Jesus Christ has been and always will be in my life, my family, and my business. He has taught me that I am to put Him first and others second, before myself, in operating my business. Christ made the ultimate sacrifice for me, and I think we, as corporate leaders, can at least follow His example by making necessary sacrifices for the benefit of those who make our corporations successful—our employees.

"God put each of us on earth, not to live a joyless life working 14 hours a day just to put food on the table for those we love and care for. His love applies to everyone from the factory worker to the CEO. He loves us all equally," BB paused.

"He cannot love any one of us more than the other. God plays no favorites! None of us is worthless in the eyes of the Lord our God. One of the wisest CEO's on earth, a man named Solomon said, 'Wealth is worthless in the day of wrath.' When Jesus keeps His promise to return, He and He alone will decide your worthiness to enter heaven and enjoy eternal life where there will be no sickness, no pain, no worries, no hardships—your only task will be to love the Lord your God with all your heart and with all your soul and with all your mind. Today, right now in fact, all you need to do is surrender your life to Jesus. Ask Him to come into your life and forgive you where you have fallen short. Accept Him as your only God and Savior, and you will have eternal life. Is it worth it? Only you can decide."

Sarah could not understand a word BB said. She was amazed that this wonderful man she was married to could speak Chinese. She thought back to the day their lives were forever changed at the revival and remembered how the Hispanic couple were talking back and forth in English and Spanish. At that time he had told her, "One thing I want to do if I ever get the chance is to learn another language and be able to really communicate well with it." *But how in the world did he ever learn Mandarin well enough to be able to give this speech?* she wondered.

She looked around the convention center to see only deadpan looks on those BB was trying to reach. They were showing customary Chinese courtesy in hearing him out, but would probably leave the arena, go home, and forget what they had heard, or at least that is what she thought.

After another few minutes William concluded his speech. He realized there could be no altar call in the

Beijing International Convention Center, so he gave them not only a website they could access to indicate that they had come to Christ, but also a means by which they could send a text message. He implored his viewers that, with all the turmoil in the world today, they needed to accept Jesus Christ as their Lord and Savior as quickly as possible. "Take a chance; take a leap of faith. It's your life; it's your soul. He's the only Son of the Most High God—accept Him now!"

William bowed to his audience as he thanked them for the opportunity to share his Lord and Savior, Jesus Christ, with them.

It was obvious that those in attendance were stunned by his message. No one was permitted to talk about Jesus Christ openly in China. This man had certainly broken Chinese law.

A nervous Mr. Kim Khiang Wee moved toward the podium in a quandary. He knew he had to fulfill his duties as emcee and thank William for his speech, but he wasn't sure how to approach the man who had just transgressed the law. Above all, he was determined to save face for International Asian Machinery for suggesting what had turned out to be a fiasco.

As Wee neared the front of the stage, a subordinate of his ran to BB, dropped to his knees, and cried out, "I want to be the first to accept Jesus Christ as my Lord and Savior! Count me as number one!"

It was as if a large vacuum had sucked the air out of the auditorium. Mr. Wee stood helpless, knowing full well no corrective measure could be taken on national television.

Understanding just enough Mandarin to guess what was going on, William reached down and helped the newly born Christian to his feet and said, "Please do not bow before me, bow only before Jesus Christ. I am only the messenger." Realizing the dangerous position in which the man had just placed himself, William bowed his head respectfully toward him and said, "It is a courageous and honorable decision for you to risk everything to have a relationship with Jesus Christ. God's peace be with you. " He hoped the tone of his voice would cross the language barrier.

The cameras panned the audience as a means to show their disapproval of BB's speech. Then it happened. A Chinese industrial magnate stood, raised his hands, and yelled out, "Come into my heart, Lord Jesus, become my Lord and Savior! Find me in this miserable world. Make me whole." Slowly, a few hundred of China's corporate executives stood and proclaimed Jesus as their Lord and Savior, asking for God's forgiveness.

William was shocked, but elated. At least a few had heard and understood the truth.

Sarah and LC were in awe of what they had just witnessed. "What will happen to these converts?" she whispered.

"My guess is nothing," LC replied. "Since this was on national TV, it will be picked up by major news outlets all over the world by morning. The Chinese cannot put themselves in a position where they will look intolerant. I think that fellow standing next to William has created his own Tiananmen Square. But instead of staring down tanks, he's put his life at risk by looking down the barrel of the cannon of Chinese history and theocracy right here in the BICC, and he did it without blinking. I guess we can call this a good old Mexican standoff right here in Beijing," LC started to laugh at the humor yet irony of his statement.

"You know, Sarah, it's only been a few years since I saw the light of Jesus Christ, and tonight I am virtually blinded by His presence. Let's go back to meet the man of the hour."

"Not until you explain what placing his hand in his pocket means."

"Oh, that!" He raised his eyebrow as if he were going to reveal a secret. "I'll explain as we walk. As you know, BB was concerned that even though he had the promise of the Chinese government that they would not edit his speech in any way and that it would be telecast live, there was a good possibility they might shut down the translators somehow. You know how BB has a penchant for detail. Well, he decided to learn Chinese. Now, that my dear lady is one tall order. Chinese is, if not the most difficult language to speak on earth, one of the most difficult. And to learn to speak it in less than a year is very ambitious. BB knew that my department had the expertise to help him, so we gave him our top level course. Even though he is a quick learner, he could not master the language well enough to give a full blown speech like tonight, but he did learn it to a degree that he could repeat a sentence by sentence translation of his speech so that it sounded like he was speaking fluent Chinese. He worked with Tony Hall on the English version; my people translated it."

LC took Sarah's arm and guided her through a doorway to a connecting hall as they continued to walk. "Tony came up with the idea of an 'ear prompt' which is a wireless device that looks like a hearing aid that can be placed in the ear. An MP3 player with the speech already on it was then placed in his pocket, but William had to…"

"Push the button to get it started!" Sarah finished his sentence. "How ingenious!"

"But that should not detract from the difficulty of what he did. Even with help, BB pulled off a minor miracle."

When Sarah and LC entered the room backstage where William was waiting for them, there was a strange look on his face and his eyes were moist. He took Sarah in his arms and drew her close as he choked back tears.

"Grammy's gone."

"How do you know?" Sarah cried.

"I just got the text message."

Sarah started to weep.

William faltered, "Now I understand why it was so important to her to know we would all be together in heaven someday…she knew this day would eventually come."

Wiping away Sarah's tears with his handkerchief, he said, "I think it's time for us to go. Can we leave now, LC?"

"Your wish is my command," LC said. "Your luggage is on the plane, and the flight plans have been filed. All we have to do is get there in one piece." He nodded to the CIA security detail that was now surrounding them.

"My best diplomatic guess is that our hosts are not too pleased with you, William J. Brantley, so let's get out of here pronto."

"Not before we thank Him who got us safely this far," BB said as he held Sarah's hand in one and reached for LC's with the other. The rest of the American group followed suit and formed a prayer circle. They thanked God for his blessing on this momentous endeavor and asked for His efforts through them to be fruitful and for a safe trip home.

Chapter 10

The Results

"Closet Christian, that's what you would have called a Chinese Christian before tonight," LC began as he looked across the jet's compartment at Sarah curled up on the couch, her head on BB's lap. "Before tonight, if you admitted you were a Christian, you and your whole family more than likely would have ended up in prison or worse. Now, with the whole world watching, it could change."

"I pray you're right," BB said over the drone of the jet's engines as they headed home.

The small group was exhausted, but too excited about the evening's event to sleep. They talked about BB's little surprise of being able to give the speech in Mandarin and the use of his ear prompt.

"I have one bummer for you guys," LC said. "The Chinese were not as hospitable as we thought, that is the politicians and corporate leaders. Through a contact in Beijing, one of my men found out that there may have been plans to get the information they wanted one way

114

or the other. I guess the bright side is we were one step ahead of them with Tom Dussell's 'red herrings.' They actually think they got it all through their surveillance devices."

Sarah and BB looked at each other in thankful relief, knowing that their prayers for God's protection had been fully answered.

The night lingered on as they kept in constant touch with Tom Dussell and Tony Hall to see if William's speech had any affect. Twelve hours later, there were a few internet responses, about enough to match the "altar call" at BICC.

"Let's not put the cart before the horse," Tony reminded them it might take time. "It's only been 12 hours since you gave the speech. You have to give it time to sink in."

From the tone of Tony's voice, BB recognized that he too was also concerned.

"BB. BB, wake up!" LC's voice seemed to be calling from the opposite end of a long tunnel.

"Where am I?" a groggy BB mumbled.

"About 35,000 feet over Alaska."

"Alaska!" BB snapped to. "How long have I been out?" He looked down and Sarah was still sleeping on his lap.

"A little over three hours," LC replied. "You have to see this!" He turned up the sound on the television. Major news networks were broadcasting live from

Tiananmen Square with many of the announcers saying the same thing.

"There are, by our best estimate, over 150,000 people crammed into Tiananmen Square, raising lighted candles, all professing to have accepted Jesus as their Lord and Savior as a result of a nationally televised speech at the Beijing International Convention Center by the renowned manufacturing mogul, William J. Brantley. The Chinese police are out in full force but so far have done little more than crowd control. If anything, they seem to be focusing on that man who first professed his faith to Brantley while still in the Convention Center. He seems to show no fear and is leading the throng in a short chant, followed by the crowd singing a few words."

"How beautiful!" a sleepy Sarah said as she was awakened by the excitement.

"There are reports of many other such demonstrations of equal size going on throughout China," the reporter exclaimed, "places where we can't even get our cameras." The television showed as many scenes as they had available to them, all with candlelight vigils and singing.

"Mr. Dussell's on the line," one of LC's men said.

"BB, how does 74,122,456 hits and growing from China sound to you? The counter looks like the dollar signs when you're pumping gas. We should be past 80 million before the hour is up!" Tom said.

"It's exciting, but not quite a billion, Tom," BB reminded him.

"Where's your faith, BB? We've just begun. Look at

the numbers from the rest of the world. It's like a spreading computer virus, and the more media coverage the better. As the rest of the world wakes up to the news and your speech is translated into more and more languages—it's going to happen, my friend. It's going to happen."

For the next two days, BB and Sarah made the arrangements for Grammy's funeral and burial, thankful to have corporate chaplain Tom Shaffer caring for them every step of the way. Tom's training enabled him to understand and empathize with the very mixed emotions BB had at the tremendous loss of Grammy combined with the exhilaration and exhaustion from his trip.

The rest of the team watched the growing numbers in Tom Dussell's computer lab. Asian countries other than China had registered close to 350 million in the first 24 hours. North, South and Latin America numbered well over 100 million within 36 hours. Europe, the Baltics, and the former Soviet Union were slow to respond, but reached 137 million within 39 hours. The totals were a little over 662 million just 50 hours after William's speech, at which point the numbers began to slow to a trickle. By 70 hours, the count reached a little over 896 million and slowed to a virtual halt.

At 71 hours the entire team gathered in B & A's large conference room drinking any caffeine they could find. They were all dressed in their Sunday best to attend Grammy's funeral service in two hours, where Tony would deliver the eulogy and Tom would present the Gospel to what was expected to be a capacity congregation.

"Not quite a billion," Tony repeated BB's words. "It was a lofty goal and we almost made it. Think about all of those saved souls for Christ out there, from just one speech. I salute all of you for such a gallant effort, but most of all I thank God for this miracle He has performed and allowed us to be a part of."

Andrew White stood patiently in the room's open door frame, his arms crossed, a sheaf of papers in his hand, as Tony gave his soliloquy.

Andrew spoke up in a mocking, I-told-you-so tone of voice, "Oh ye of little faith!"

Every set of eyes turned to look at him. He held up the papers in his hand. "You forgot Africa. Not one of you said anything about Africa, and since my parents are missionaries there I thought I'd take it upon myself to track African numbers just to see how they compare. How does 203,004,696 sound? Now that does not count the two to three thousand converts from my parents, of course."

Tom Dussell was furiously calculating on a yellow legal pad. "1,096,406,096 give or take a few, but who's counting? We are!"

"Hallelujah," Tony screamed as loudly as he could. "One billion ninety-six million, four hundred six thousand and what?"

"And ninety-six, sorry ninety-seven, oops, ninety-eight....."

The whole room burst into laughter.

William grabbed Sarah and twirled her around as if on a dance floor, then kissed her. "Thank you for supporting me through all of this." He turned and waved his hand to indicate everyone in the room. "And thanks to all of you."

Everyone applauded. They formed a circle and praised God for they recognized that this was truly His work, not theirs. "And we can't stop here, Lord. We ask that You would send out those who are to shepherd this new flock and the resources they will need. In the bold and precious name of Jesus we pray. Amen."

"Amen," they all responded with LC adding his own personal postscript, "Lord, I think you'd better get Noah building quite a few more rooms in Your mansion in heaven."

They all responded with a laugh and "Amen!"

Chapter 11

The Next Steps

The events that took place in the lives of BB, Sarah, and the hundreds of millions of people in our story is something that can take place in the life of every person. In fact, it is something God wants to see happen. The God of the universe is interested not only in the events of this world, but also the events of *your* life. God was aware of the day of your birth, and it is His desire to see a second day of birth—a spiritual birth—happen in your life.

This truth is one BB became acutely aware of the night he and Sarah attended the Tony Hall meeting. BB received the truth of John 3:16 for his own life that night, and many years later as he spoke to a Chinese television audience he was able to impart that truth to the world. John 3:16 says, "For God so loved the world that he gave his one and only Son, that whoever believes in him shall not perish but have eternal life" (NIV).

So what exactly happened in the lives of BB, Sarah, and the one billion others? They all experienced what the Bible calls "new birth." The Bible teaches that we all need to experience and celebrate two birthdays. If you are reading this sentence, you have experienced the first birth—the physical birth that occurred when you passed from your mother's womb and made your entrance into this world. The second birthday is a spiritual birth and one Jesus spoke of during a conversation with a leader named Nicodemus.

It is interesting to note the number of leaders Jesus seemed to attract during his short time of ministry. Perhaps it was because He ran a thriving carpentry business himself. Perhaps His messages struck a chord with those who had achieved earthly success but found it empty. Nevertheless, the New Testament provides a record of many successful people, people just like BB and Sarah, magnetically drawn to the life-changing Good News that Jesus offered.

Nicodemus, a leader certainly looked up to by many, approached Jesus with far more questions than answers. He surrendered his pride and his position for a singular pursuit—a personal encounter with Jesus Christ. Perhaps you're reading this book with the same attitude Nicodemus had when he approached Jesus. Nicodemus recognized Jesus as a great leader and came to Him with words of praise for His wonderful works. He said, "Rabbi, we know you are a teacher who has come from God. For no one could perform the miraculous signs you are doing if God were not with him" (John 3:2 NIV).

Perhaps like Nicodemus you know instinctively there is just something different about this man named Jesus you've heard so much about. Perhaps like Nicodemus, and just like the hero of our story, BB, you know there has to be something more about Him than just a few good teachings, a few good works, and a few good morals. Perhaps you've had a family member, someone like Idella, telling you there is something more to be discovered about this man called Jesus.

While Nicodemus' words were true, they missed the real mark. Jesus' response to Nicodemus was a pointed change of subject. The New Testament records, "In reply Jesus declared, 'I tell you the truth, no one can see the kingdom of God unless he is born again'" (John 3:3 NIV). Jesus brings the real mark into clear focus with a very direct and challenging statement sure to capture the attention of a mover and shaker like Nicodemus. No one goes to heaven unless he is born again. No one "gets in good with God" unless he is born again. No one fixes what is broken about his life unless he is born again. But what do these words "born again" really mean?

Your personal reaction to these two words could vary. You could respond negatively, based on your preconceived notions of people described as "born again believers." Or perhaps your search for the meaning of these words could be like that of Nicodemus, who responded with confusion and even more questions. While either response would be natural, the words of Jesus contain supernatural meaning. The Bible records this supernatural truth to his very natural response.

> *In reply Jesus declared, "I tell you the truth, no one can see the kingdom of God unless he is born again."*

"How can a man be born when he is old?"
Nicodemus asked, "Surely he cannot enter a
second time into his mother's womb to be born!"

Jesus answered, "I tell you the truth, no one
can enter the kingdom of God unless he is born
of water and the Spirit. Flesh gives birth to
flesh, but the Spirit gives birth to spirit" (John
3:3-6, NIV).

In other words, no one gets into heaven without experiencing two birthdays—a physical birthday first and
then a spiritual one. Right now as you read the words on
this page, a supernatural work may be occurring in your
life. It's the same work that occurred in the life of
Nicodemus over 2000 years ago, and the same work that
occurred in the life of BB. The Spirit may be giving birth
to your spirit. While this work may be supernatural, it is
not complicated. Because the work is supernatural, you
and I bring nothing but ourselves to the birthday party.

The night BB and Sarah visited the revival tent, they
recognized what Nicodemus recognized. They recognized what is true of every human being. They saw that
we are all spiritually dead because of sin and recognized
sin for what it really is—an attempt to run life on our
own terms, independent of God. In essence, sin is you
and I saying to God, "You run the world, and I'll run my
own life." They also recognized the penalty for their sin,
and at the same time the solution. The penalty and the
solution are summarized beautifully in one verse found

in the New Testament book of Romans. Romans 6:23 states,

> *For the wages of sin is death, but the gift of God*
> *is eternal life in Christ Jesus our Lord* (NIV).

Like any gift, God's gift of life in and through Jesus is a gift to be received. It was a gift that required BB, Sarah, Nicodemus, and hundreds of million others throughout history to move beyond recognition to throw their arms wide to receive the gift so freely offered by God. Jesus Christ and what He did on the cross is the gift you receive on your spiritual birthday. He paid for all our sins so that we could spend eternity with God in heaven.

Perhaps this book was a gift from a friend. Perhaps for the first time you are recognizing that you need a brand new birthday—a spiritual birthday. The night BB and Sarah visited the tent was the night they moved from recognition to reception. The night BB spoke to his Chinese audience was the night hundreds of millions began the move from recognition to reception. Perhaps today is the day for you to move from recognition to reception. Listen to the New Testament words of 2 Corinthians 6:2.

> *For God says, "At just the right time, I heard*
> *you. On the day of salvation, I helped you."*
> *Indeed, God is ready to help you right now.*
> *Today is the day of salvation* (NLT).

Wherever you are reading this, I invite you to bow your head and voice a simple prayer to God that will change your life forever. You can pray the following prayer right now:

> Jesus, I want a spiritual birthday. I know that I am a sinner without help apart from You. I believe that only You can save me from my sins, so please come into my life. I believe that You died on my behalf at the cross; You went to the grave and rose again. Father, I come to You alone with my sins and ask for forgiveness because I know I have disobeyed You throughout my entire life. Only You have the power to change me. I praise You for sending Your only Son to save me. From now on my life belongs to You, so that whether I die right now, tomorrow, or whenever, I know I will be with You in heaven for eternity. Let me live for You all the days of my life, I pray in Christ's name. Amen.

If you sincerely prayed this prayer, let me be the first to say, happy birthday! Let me encourage you to write today's date on this page and let this page be your spiritual birth certificate. While I'm passing out encouragement, let me make one final suggestion. Share the news of your spiritual birthday with someone else, perhaps the person who gave you this book.

Guess what else is going on right now if you just prayed that prayer? Well, the Bible states in Luke 15:10:

*In the same way, I tell you, there is joy in the
presence of the angels of God over one sinner
who repents* (NASB).

In other words, the angels in heaven are at this very
moment holding a spiritual birthday party just for you.

Here's one more thing for you to think about following your decision for a spiritual birthday. Just as
your name was written down on your birth certificate at
the hospital on the day of your physical birth, God has
now written down your name on a spiritual birth certificate in what the Bible calls the "Book of Life of the
Lamb" (Revelation 13:8 NKJV). And here is some really
great news, your name is written in this book in the in-
erasable blood of Jesus so that it can never be removed.
Take time right now to start your prayer conversation
with God by talking to Him, thanking Him for what He
has just done in your life.

Now He wants you to go out and tell someone else
what has just happened in your life. Be bold like the
Chinese business people who risked their futures and
possibly their lives and stood for Jesus at the conference
following BB's speech. Jesus spoke directly to this point
in the New Testament Gospel of Mark 8:38 when He
said:

*For whoever is ashamed of Me and My words in
this adulterous and sinful generation, of him the
Son of Man also will be ashamed when He
comes in the glory of His Father with the holy
angels* (NKJV).

What Christian in their right mind would ever want Jesus to be ashamed of them? Of course, no one would, so don't be afraid to tell others that you have turned from your sin and trusted Jesus alone to be your Lord and Savior. Who knows, He may use your words to usher hundreds of millions into a real and vibrant relationship with Him.

Why not start now? You can visit our website, www.iamchap.org and click the "Awakening" button to let us know about your decision. We will not share your address information with anyone else, but we may send you free material that will help you get started off right in your Christian walk.

Afterword

So there you have it, a billion new converts in 72 hours. Could this or anything remotely like it really happen? Well, God really did create the heavens and earth in six days, didn't He? Could a third great awakening really come about this simply? Years ago, as I studied the life of Jesus and His statements in the New Testament, I came to realize that His genius was often displayed in the simplest of phrases:

"Follow me and I will make you fishers of men."

"Blessed are the pure in heart for they shall see God."

"I have come not to destroy, but to fulfill."

How about His giving us the perfect prayer to speak to God the Father that contains less than 65 words? Yes, Jesus demonstrated time and again that the most complicated of subjects could be reduced to the radically sublime in only a few words from God. So why is it so far-fetched that He might bring more than a billion people into relationship with Himself in just a few days? Just think for a moment about the prophecy of Joel from Acts 2:16-21 (NLT):

> *No, what you see this morning was predicted centuries ago by the prophet Joel: "In the last days, God said, I will pour out my Spirit upon all people. Your sons and daughters will prophesy, your young men will see visions, and your old men will dream dreams. In those days*

I will pour out my Spirit upon all my servants, men and women alike, and they will prophesy. And I will cause wonders in the heavens above and signs on the earth below—blood and fire and clouds of smoke. The sun will be turned into darkness, and the moon will turn blood red before that great and glorious day of the Lord arrives. And anyone who calls on the name of the Lord will be saved."

Amazing things happen all the time, and we don't give it a second thought. As I am writing this, three powerful hurricanes have hit the state of Florida in the same month and should have wiped out whole cities. Even though much personal property has been destroyed, millions of lives have been spared. The same God, who holds the wind and waves in check, can and will pour out His Spirit, and a third great awakening may well result. If you are someone who enters the workplace on a regular basis, take an awakening mentality with you to work from this day forward. Be ready to share the story of the two birthdays from chapter eleven with friends at work. Ask God to commission you as a workplace missionary and study His Word, searching for ways to share His love, power, forgiveness, and hope in your very special mission field. Never forget that the seeds of every great movement of God begin with a single person, and that person just may be you.

Lastly, what should you do if you are business leader with a true desire to see an awakening in the workplace? Here are few tips:

Pray that God will bring you out in the open about your faith and use you as an agent of change that just may usher in the *Third Awakening*.

Be sensitive to the spiritual needs of your employees, and be ready at any moment, with their permission, to share the Good News.

Bring a corporate chaplain on the team to help you care for the employees. Although they are not the only organizations working in this area, two respected national agencies that stand ready to help in this area are:

Marketplace Ministries at
www.marketplaceministries.com
and
Corporate Chaplains of America at
www.iamchap.org.

Continue to grow in your relationship with Christ by being active in a strong, biblically sound church.

Contact your local FCCI chapter and get active. More information can be found at **www.fcci.org**.

Join a C-12 Group in your area. More information can be found at **www.thec12group.com**.

Familiarize yourself with the work of Os Hillman and use his books, conferences, and resources. More information can be found at **www.marketplaceleaders.org**.

There are hundreds of other valid workplace ministry organizations in America. Here is a small sampling of some sites that will link you to many others:

Crown Financial Ministries – **www.crown.org**
Priority Associates – **www.priorityassociates.org**
CBMC International – **www.cbmcint.org**
BBL Forum – **www.bblforum.com**

Find other business leaders in your area with whom to network and share fellowship.

Encourage your pastor and others at church to see the workplace as a platform for ministry and fruitful mission field.

Take every possible step to position your company as a platform for ministry. Remember the prophet who said today is like a "mist that dries up..." but eternity is forever.

Develop an awakening mentality in all that you do.

Pray for an awakening to come through the workplace.

God, please give us a third great awakening, let it begin in the workplace, and by all means let us see it in our lifetime. Amen.